Praise for *Cross My* THE HIDDEN DIARY,

Cross My Heart was *very* descriptive (but not, like, overloaded!) and fun. It's a touching story that a lot of girls can relate to because of their own busy parents. I liked the mystery, too!

> Lilly, eleven years old, daughter of Liz Curtis Higgs,
> author of *Bad Girls of the Bible*

Mama mia! *Cross My Heart* was a great book! I liked the way the author left you hanging at the end of each chapter. It made you want to keep reading. I could really relate to some of the characters, and Claudette made me laugh. You'll love this book! Cross my heart!

> Tavia, ten years old, daughter of Deborah Raney,
> author of *A Vow to Cherish* and *Beneath a Southern Sky*

This book was really good, interesting, and fun. I couldn't say I had one favorite part because I loved the whole book! I couldn't put it down.

> Tyler, eleven years old, daughter of Lisa E. Samson,
> author of *The Church Ladies*

I couldn't put this book down! I guarantee you'll love *Cross My Heart,* and it will keep you on the edge of your seat.

> Marie, thirteen years old, daughter of Terri Blackstock,
> author of the NEWPOINTE 911 series

Cross My Heart is a very exciting book. Lucy... meets new friends and learns about God. I know my friends will love this book like I did. Maybe we'll find a hidden diary somewhere, too.

> Madelyn, nine years old, daughter of Cindy McCormick
> Martinusen, author of *Winter Passing*

I think Lucy and Serena are really cool. I can't wait to read the next HIDDEN DIARY book.

> Bethany, nine years old, daughter of Janet Holm McHenry,
> author of *PrayerWalk* and *Girlfriend Gatherings*

Books by
Sandra Byrd
FROM BETHANY HOUSE PUBLISHERS

Girl Talk
The Inside-Out Beauty Book

THE HIDDEN DIARY
Cross My Heart
Make a Wish
Just Between Friends
Take a Bow
Pass It On
Change of Heart
Take a Chance
One Plus One

THE
HIDDEN
DIARY

7

Take a Chance

SANDRA BYRD

BETHANYHOUSE

MINNEAPOLIS, MINNESOTA

Published by Bethany House Publishers
A Ministry of Bethany Fellowship International
11400 Hampshire Avenue South
Bloomington, Minnesota 55438
www.bethanyhouse.com

Printed in the United States of America by
Bethany Press International, Bloomington, Minnesota 55438

Library of Congress Cataloging-in-Publication Data

Byrd, Sandra.
    Take a chance / by Sandra Byrd.
        p.   cm. — (The hidden diary ; bk. 7)
Summary: Lucy and Serena look for a way to save the financially strapped Double C horse ranch and its Country Cousins program for child riders.
    ISBN 0-7642-2486-7 (pbk.)
    [1. Horses—Fiction. 2. Diaries—Fiction. 3. Santa Catalina Island (Calif.)—Fiction. 4. Christian life—Fiction.] I. Title.
    PZ7.B9898 Tam   2002
    [Fic]—dc21
                                                 2002008837

For

Sam Byrd

Contents

Double C

Saturday afternoon . . . D Day minus six

"Why won't this crazy thing stand up?" Lucy stuck the shaft of the open umbrella into a cowboy boot. It tipped to the side, but at least it didn't fall over.

"Quick!" Serena dived underneath the teetering umbrella. "We've got, like, two minutes. My mom's going to holler upstairs for us any second. Since she's so busy helping my dad this week, if we're not ready when she is, she might call off the whole idea!"

The girls always read the old diary under the yellow beach umbrella. Normally it was stuck into the sand at the beach. But this time they were in Serena's room.

Lucy scooted under the umbrella, her heart racing.

Serena cracked open the Hidden Diary. At the beginning of the summer the girls had found this diary, written in 1932 by Serena's great-grandmother and her best friend, Mary. Each week Lucy and Serena read a section of the old diary and did something just like the 1932 girls had done during the section they read. No matter what. They'd read yesterday what the diary girls planned that week—horseback riding—but not what adventure awaited.

"Dearest Diary," Lucy started reading Mary's curly handwriting.

"I've got the most wonderful news. They've brought horses over from the mainland for the summer—isn't that grand! And this week promises a wonderful treat. Serena and I will be riding two big stallions this week!"

Stallions! Lucy had never ridden a stallion. Were they dangerous? She handed the diary over to Serena, who began to read her great-grandmother's blocky handwriting.

"mary thinks we're riding them. I myself have doubts. They're very big, and Joey says they're unbroken. We haven't even been invited to ride them in any case. You know mary; she's scheming already, trying to get us on those horses, buttering up anyone who can help. I've bet her she can't get us a ride and she's bet me we can. If she gets us one, I must ride with her even though I am fearful. If not, she must promise to stop asking for the rest of the summer."

Serena handed the diary back to Lucy, who read the last curly loops.

"Diary, you wait and see. I'll wangle us both a ride on those stallions, together, before the end of the week."

Serena finished with,

"Let's just hope she gets us off of them in one piece, Diary! I'm a bit frightened. More later.
Faithful Friends,
mary and Serena."

Lucy closed the diary. "Does Carla have stallions?" she asked with a smile. Carla owned the Double C Ranch, where they were going to ride today.

Serena giggled and shook her head from side to side. "You brave heart. When's the last time you rode a stallion?"

"Umm . . . never."

"Uh-huh. And when's the last time you rode *any* kind of horse?" Serena said, closing the umbrella.

"Last spring," Lucy said. "I really loved it. I'm an animal person, you know. Since I'm an only child, pets are like brothers and sisters to me."

"Let's see what's happening at Carla's, okay?" Serena took the umbrella out of the boot and then hopped around on one foot trying to slide the boot on.

"Okay," Lucy answered. *I'm going to ride one. I will. I must.* She smiled. Then she fished into her jeans pocket. "Oh yeah, come here a sec." Serena came close, and Lucy twisted a ponytail holder with a small daisy around the bottom of each of Serena's short, dark brown braids. Then she twisted two around her own strawberry-blond braids. "I got a whole pack of these. I thought they'd be fun for us riding."

"Thanks!" Serena said. The girls stared at themselves in the mirror, then stuck their tongues out and started giggling at their reflections. Lucy swiped her hand across the top of her nose, wishing the freckles would wipe off. Serena had such smooth brown skin.

"Serena! Hurry up! Let's go!" Serena's mom called upstairs. Lucy watched as Serena grabbed a picture of herself as a younger girl from inside her top desk drawer. Then they scurried down and into the car borrowed for the day to take them to the interior.

"Stallions, here I come!" Lucy whispered under her breath.

The town of Avalon melted behind them, its rocky coastline fading behind the rear window and the mountains of the interior growing larger as they drove toward them. Catalina Island was twenty-six miles off the coast of Los Angeles, but it was like nowhere else Lucy had ever been, and she was here for the whole summer with her new best friend, Serena.

"I hope Carla's taking care of herself," Serena's mother said as they drove toward the ranch. "Ever since Cal died, she's been trying to keep that place up on her own."

"Carla's husband died two years ago," Serena whispered.

"She's got those Country Cousins kids there two weeks out of the month. I think it's a lot for her." Mrs. Romero flipped on her blinker even though there wasn't another car in sight. Then she turned onto the dusty country road that led to the ranch.

"Carla loves the Country Cousins kids," Serena reminded her mother. "They'd never get to leave Los Angeles and ride in the fresh air if it weren't for people like Carla."

"Yes," her mom agreed.

Lucy watched the edge of the road as they drove along, and soon a fence appeared. The split-rail wood had been painted once, but the merciless sun had bleached out the paint almost entirely. Lucy felt her palm. If she ran her hand along that fence, she'd end up with a bouquet of slivers. *Ouch.*

Soon they came to the gate. Above the entrance were two capital letter *C*s facing each other.

"The Double C Ranch," Mrs. Romero said. "I used to tease Carla that those letter *C*s were kissing each other, for her and for Cal."

"I'm sure she loved that!" Serena joked. She turned to Lucy. "Carla is, like, totally a rancher. No fancy stuff. No emotional smoochy stuff. No sobby stuff."

Lucy looked at the double *C*s. They kind of looked like a broken heart. "Maybe they mean Country Cousins now," she said. "I mean, since her husband died."

"Yeah," Serena said. "She does love them. They come out each day for a couple of weeks. They go home each night on the ferry while Carla rests up. She's ready for them when they arrive the next morning."

They pulled up in front of the barn. "I didn't call ahead," Mrs. Romero said, "since Carla usually says not to bother." The girls got out of the car. The red paint on the huge barn was fading, like the paint on the fences. It looked like a real ranch. As they stepped into the barn, Lucy closed her eyes and treated her nose to the dry country perfume of the hay.

"Whoa!" Lucy's eyes flew open as she was almost knocked over. A baby pig, its curly tail looking like a pasta salad noodle, bumped her legs and feet, squeaking as it ran by.

Mrs. Romero went into the office with Carla, who had just said good-bye to the Country Cousins and left her ranch hand to see them off. Lucy and Serena ran to look at the horses.

Lucy scanned quickly for stallions. Would she know one by sight?

Most of the kids were out near the van ready to go, but two little ones were still brushing their horses.

"Cinnamon and Sugar!" Serena said, pointing to the horses.

Lucy walked over to the rusty horse, patted her flank, and said, "Hi," to a girl with strawberry-blond braids just like Lucy's.

"My name is Sal," the girl said. "I love your daisy

braids. This is my horse, Cinnamon. I don't want to leave her." Sal smiled toward the brown-haired girl brushing out the blond horse. "That's my best friend, Susan," she said.

Serena patted the head of the brown-haired girl. "Can I help?"

The girl nodded her head, and Serena helped her finish brushing out Sugar's coat.

Lucy lifted Sal back onto the horse. "Just once more," Sal had whispered. "So I can remember for always what it feels like." Sal's laughter filled the barn like the swallows' birdsong, and Lucy laughed right along with her. Then she lifted her down so Sal could gather her belongings and get ready to leave the ranch with the rest of the Country Cousins.

Serena smiled. "I learned to ride right here on this ranch with the Country Cousins. On a horse named Whisper, who was the mother of Cinnamon and Sugar."

"Come on, guys!" Little Sal and Susan tugged Lucy and Serena toward the entrance to the barn, where they were loading the van. "We're having Popsicles before we go!"

"Did you ever notice that when you're having fun time goes fast, and when you're not it goes slow?" Susan asked, peeling the wrapper off her treat.

Serena nodded. Lucy handed a napkin to Sal, whose Popsicle was already melting down the sides like a candle.

Sal licked the drips and said, "I wish I never had to

leave here. Popsicles taste better in the country."

After a few minutes the girls helped Brad, the ranch hand, get the Country Cousins loaded into the van. Sal held on to Lucy's hand. "I wish I didn't have to go. I love horses. My mom didn't have enough money for me to ride one. But Country Cousins doesn't make you pay anything, so kids like me can come. Isn't that great?"

Lucy's heart squeezed. She felt like hugging Sal, but instead she reached up and unwound the two daisy wraps from around her braids. One by one, she slid them over Sal's pigtails. "Now you can remember the ranch and remember me."

Sal took off her red bandanna and handed it to Lucy. "Here's a present for you, then. Take good care of Cinnamon for me."

Their van pulled out in a cloud of dust, heading toward the ferry and home. Serena turned toward Lucy. "Cinnamon and Sugar are sisters. I love Sugar the best. We could probably ride them today, too, if we wanted."

Hmm. Had Serena forgotten about the stallions? Lucy really wanted a big stallion, like in the movies, especially because the diary girls were doing that. But it seemed clear that Serena wanted them to ride Cinnamon and Sugar together.

Should she say something? Lucy really wanted Serena to be happy. But she really wanted to ride a stallion, too.

"Let's ask Carla if it's okay to ride," Serena said.

She knocked on the office door.

Serena's mom slowly opened it.

The girls stepped into the office. As they did, Carla lifted her head from her hands.

Non-smoochy, non-sobby, unemotional Carla was crying.

Reel Filmworks

Saturday afternoon . . .

"I'm sorry." Carla blew her nose and shoved a stack of envelopes into another stack of envelopes, like shuffling an extra-large deck of cards. "It's the bills." She pulled a cloth handkerchief out of her pocket and blew her nose in it, then folded it and stuck it back into her pocket.

"Is there any way I can help?" Serena's mom asked.

"I don't think so," Carla said. "I think I've just let the last batch of Country Cousins kids go. I just can't afford to keep doing it." She sighed. "I've worked hard to keep the ranch going after Cal passed on."

Lucy looked at the wall behind Carla's desk. There was a big bulletin board with lots of kids' pictures taped and tacked together in a collage—Country Cousins kids.

A smaller bulletin board had a picture of a younger

Carla and a man in their wedding clothes in a horse-drawn carriage. There was also a black-and-white picture of a little girl with two missing teeth and freckles like stardust sprinkled across her nose. Their daughter?

"There must be some way!" Serena's mom said.

"I've tried to keep up with the bills by renting the stallions out . . ."

Stallions! Lucy thought.

" . . . and offering rides in the hills for the tourists. But I'm kind of off the beaten path." Carla shuffled the bills on her desk again. "Bill Bixson's got that frilly ranch in town now, and he's listed in all the directories. He does send me his overflow customers from time to time. I can't decide if he does it because he's really nice or just to rub it in that he's got extras." Carla sniffled again. "No, that's not kind of me to say. Sorry. I'm just worked up."

Silence ticked by.

"We came to ride," Mrs. Romero finally said. "But maybe this isn't a good time?"

Carla shook her head. "The horses are tired from those little ones here all week, and I need to call the banker and see what I can do with my payments. I've got to call Country Cousins headquarters and tell them the kids probably can't come in August. I can't have kids on the property. Need to keep it neat and tidy once it's listed for sale."

"For sale?!" Serena and her mother said at once.

Carla's eyes teared up again. "Now, don't get me started. I'd better get on the phone. Why don't you come back tomorrow afternoon and the girls can ride then."

Serena nodded, her lips pressed together to stop the quiver. Lucy felt so awful to see her so upset that she put her arm around Serena as they dodged the little pig on their way back to the car. Mrs. Romero had barely started the engine when Serena began to cry.

Have I ever seen Serena cry before?

Lucy reached her hand across the backseat and patted Serena's hand. "If I had a handkerchief to give you, I would," she whispered with a smile.

"Gross," Serena said, but she smiled a little through her tears.

They pulled down the driveway and past the place where Lucy had eaten Popsicles with Sal. Lucy touched the red bandanna around her neck.

"She won't really close the ranch, will she, Mom?" Serena asked.

"I guess if she has to, she has to," her mother said. "I know how much it means to her. It's all she's got left of Cal."

"And the Country Cousins!" Serena said. "They're like her kids, since she never had any."

Lucy thought of the little gap-toothed girl in the black-and-white picture in Carla's office. *Then who was that?*

"I know," Serena's mom said. "Let's pray. Lord, please let there be some way that Carla can save the ranch."

"Maybe someone could invest in the ranch," Lucy

suggested a few minutes later. "You know, a co-owner or something."

"Maybe," Serena's mom said. She sounded doubtful. "Do you guys want to go to Bill Bixson's ranch so you can ride horses today? In case Lucy's parents already have plans for tomorrow?"

Serena shrugged. "I guess so."

After cruising back into Avalon, they pulled up at a brand-new ranch. The barns were metal and shiny, the fences all painted bright red. There was a long line of people waiting to ride.

"I'm going to return this borrowed car," Serena's mom said. "I'll be back to get you in the golf cart on my way back in about an hour."

Serena and Lucy nodded and got in line behind the others.

"What's that silver stuff on the horses' tails?" Lucy asked.

"Tinfoil," Serena said. "They wrap it around their tail hairs."

"It's pretty," Lucy said. The light caught the foil and reflected back toward the girls.

"Yeah," Serena answered. "But if they took as much care as to what was good for the horses as to what looked good on the horses, it would be a lot better for the animals."

Lucy moved forward. "What do you mean?"

Serena pointed at a horse being brought up for a rider to mount. "See that saddle? It's pretty, but it doesn't fit really snug. That horse is going to be sore after a few hours of riding. I bet they bought all the saddles for one low price, but all the same size."

"Wow! I didn't know you knew so much about horses."

Serena nodded. "I usually ride more. I haven't done so much this summer because, well, you and I have been busy with other things." She smiled. "But normally I'm at Carla's once a week or so. Sometimes with Julie."

Lucy's heart dropped. Julie. For some reason known only to Julie and God, Julie had decided to hate Lucy from the moment she stepped onto Catalina Island this summer.

"Ready there, darlin'?" A man stepped up to the girls. He spit a yellow stream of tobacco juice to the side, landing just a few inches from Lucy's feet.

So much for a frilly ranch! Lucy stepped aside.

"What kind of mount would you like?"

Lucy stood tall and took a deep breath. "A stallion, please."

The tobacco man laughed out loud, his brown teeth showing. "City girl, eh? I think not. You're lucky I don't give you a donkey. How about we take this nice tame mare."

Lucy's cheeks felt hot. "I might be a city girl, but I love animals."

The man cackled. "Oh boy. Okay. The stuffed kind?"

Lucy held her tongue, got on the horse the man pointed out to her, and patted the mare's mane. The mare shifted her weight. Lucy tried to sit still in the saddle so it wouldn't hurt the mare.

"Don't worry, girl," she leaned forward and whispered toward the horse's ear. "I'm going to be easy on you. I don't want to hurt your back."

The mare shook her mane, as if she understood, and the girls began to trot toward the end of the arena. But Lucy still felt stung by the man's humiliating words.

"This certainly isn't like Carla's ranch!" Lucy said loudly to Serena. "Not as nice, not as real. Frilly."

They were just passing a man in dress pants and perfectly clean boots standing by the fence. He looked up, and he wasn't smiling. The look on his face told Lucy he had heard what she'd just said.

Lucy looked away. After she and Serena had ridden a little farther, she asked, "Who's Mr. Clean Boots?"

"Bill Bixson," Serena replied.

Uh-oh. The owner. Lucy's cheeks felt hot again.

After a few minutes the girls forgot Bill Bixson and the tobacco chewer. It was fun riding through the arena, fast and slow, then racing each other. There were lots of fenced areas to ride in, but you couldn't leave the fences and ride out toward the mountains.

"It would be fun to ride in the mountains, too," Lucy said.

"We could if we were at Carla's," Serena said.

If only there was something I could do to help Carla, Lucy thought. *To save the ranch for her—and for Serena. It means so much to Serena. And she's done so much for me since I came here this summer.*

"We'd better head back." Lucy checked her watch. "Our time is almost up."

Serena nodded. Lucy stuck her heels gently into her mount's sides. The horses raced back to the barns.

After dismounting, Lucy patted her mare and was about to lead her to some water. "Not yet," a barn hand said. "She's got to ride out one more time first."

Lucy frowned but handed the reins over.

Just as they headed out the gate, Lucy saw a van pulled up alongside the fence. The side of it said *Reel Filmworks: Bringing the World to a Screen Near You.*

"What's that?"

"Probably a film crew," Serena said. "They do a lot of movies and commercials on Catalina."

"Wow! Let's look. Maybe we'll spot someone famous!" Lucy tugged on Serena's hand.

The two of them tried to be casual, slipping up next to the van. Lucy looked around. No movie stars. At least no one that looked like one. Everyone looked . . . normal.

Too bad. She was about to tug on Serena's hand again when she overheard the crew talking.

"I guess this is about it for ranches," the tall one with the bushy mustache said. "The Island is a small place. I'd like to keep the shoot on Catalina, though, since we're doing the other one in town. It'll save money."

"Did you look up ranches before you came?" the

woman asked. Her feet looked pinched into her high heels.

"This was the only one listed. We'll bring Mickey back on Thursday to check it out and make our final decision on Friday with the rest of the crew."

Lucy leaned over and whispered into Serena's ear, "Did you hear that? They're looking for a ranch to film at."

"Sounds like they're going to film it here," Serena answered.

"I have an idea!" Lucy said. "What about Carla's ranch? I'll bet they'd pay to shoot a commercial at the ranch."

Serena's eyes lit up. "Yes! You're right!"

"Let's tell them," Lucy said.

Serena looked uncomfortable. "Will you ask?"

"Sure." Lucy walked over to the tall man. "Excuse me," she said.

They all turned to look at her.

"I'm sorry, but we overheard you were looking for a ranch. There is another ranch on Catalina. A great one. A real one."

She nudged Serena. "Tell them how to get there," she whispered.

"It's in the mountains," Serena said.

"The mountains!" The tall man smiled. "Perfect! Can you tell me where?"

Serena told him, and the man scribbled it into his day planner. "Terrific. We'll be by to check it out on Thursday afternoon, and on Friday we'll make a final decision about just what ranch to rent for our commercial shoots. Thank you, young ladies!"

Serena and Lucy clasped hands. "Rent!" Lucy whispered. "That means they're paying!"

"Shoots!" Serena said. "That means they want to film more than one thing there."

She grabbed Lucy's arm. "Uh-oh. Look who's coming."

Lucy turned and saw Mr. Clean Boots heading toward them and the film crew with long, quick steps.

Oh No!

The next morning Lucy told her parents about the great plan to save Carla's ranch.

"But right after the film crew said they would come—" Lucy slid another spoonful of cereal into her mouth and swallowed before rushing on—"Mr. Clean Boots started walking *right toward* us. I mean, fast. So Serena and I spied her mom waiting by the road and skedaddled out of there."

"Oh, Luce," her mother giggled. "You and your imagination. Maybe he just had to talk with the crew. It might not have been anything you and Serena said."

"When we rode by him earlier, you should have *seen* the look he gave me, Mom. I'm telling you the truth. And besides, don't you think a rancher with dress pants and new boots is kind of weird anyway?"

Dad tapped Lucy on the head on his way to get a final cup of coffee. "I don't suppose the sun glistened off of his gold tooth, eh?" He chuckled.

Lucy shook her head. "It's not a cartoon, Dad. Seriously." She stood up. "I'm just saying that Carla is so nice and her ranch is so real, and Serena loves it so much. I just want her to get the commercial. That's all."

"You'd better get ready for church," Mom said. "We'll visit the puppies after the service, and then I'll bring you right home so you can change before heading out to the Double C."

Lucy skedaddled upstairs and pulled a cotton dress over her head. Her strawberry-blond hair fuzzed out from static cling. She sprayed it down with water from the pink bottle meant to mist the sickly African violets on her dresser. She smoothed a tiny bead of gel into the mix and then, for a final touch—a hair band.

Just before she left her room, she ran a stick of gloss over her lips.

Ready.

They took the golf cart to church—no one drove cars in town. People who had lived there a long time, like Serena, had friends who would lend them a car whenever they needed one. Good thing, too, since they'd need one to get to the Double C later that day.

Wait till Carla hears the good news!

The sun's warmth slid in sideways and sat beside Lucy on the backseat. A minute later they parked in front of the white church with the green trim. The yellow flowers Jake had planted there that first week Lucy arrived on the Island still bloomed and, in fact, had multiplied.

Jake was sure to be in church this morning, too.

The usher showed them to their seats, but not before Lucy scanned the room to see who was there. Erica, of course. She turned and waved to Lucy as Lucy sat down. Lucy gave a happy little wave back. Jake was sitting in the row right across from them. He winked at Lucy. She blushed and winked back.

Jake was a nice guy. A really nice guy.

First they sang, Lucy's favorite part. She didn't see Rachel anywhere in the crowd. *She must be a counselor at camp again this week.* The pastor, Rachel's dad, stood up to speak. Lucy took out the notebook of purple paper she'd slipped into her Bible case and a pink Gelly Roll pen. She'd seen some other people taking notes on the sermon. And if she got really bored, she could doodle while she listened. Serena was teaching her to doodle.

While she listened, she doodled a pink pony on one sheet of paper and then made the double *C*s touch into a heart.

When the pastor spoke the Bible verse, though, Lucy jotted it down and flipped open her Bible.

" 'Pride ends in humiliation, while humility brings honor.' Proverbs 29:23," the pastor read.

Humility! I think I had enough of that at Bill Bixson's ranch yesterday! I don't think I want to feel that all the time. I felt small when that man said I should get on a donkey. She drew a picture of a small girl next to a big horse.

Lucy closed her notebook, then finished reading the section the pastor was on and listened. He sounded close to God. He didn't sound small, but he didn't sound puffed up like a rice cake, either.

After church Lucy met in the back with Erica. Jake came over to talk with them, too.

"All rested up after camp?" he asked.

"Yeah." Lucy smiled. "Serena and I are horseback riding today."

"Fun!" Erica said. "Are you coming to Power Hour tomorrow night?"

Power Hour! Lucy hadn't been to the youth group for a couple of weeks. "Sure," she said. She did feel like this was her church now, after all.

"Are you riding at Carla's?" Jake asked.

"Yes!" Lucy said. "How did you know?"

"It's a small island. I used to ride there on Fridays with my sister," Jake said.

"I know Serena's mom is friends with Carla," Erica put in.

When Jake mentioned Friday, it reminded Lucy. *This* Friday was the day that the producers would make the *final* decision. Lucy didn't feel free to mention the whole deal. Maybe Carla wanted her troubles kept private.

"I'd better go," Jake said.

"Me too," Lucy answered, hoping to get outside before Dad did something embarrassing like honk the golf cart horn. Especially because it didn't go *beep-beep*—it went *Ay-OO-ga!*

"See you tomorrow!" Erica called as Lucy jumped into the golf cart. After a quick stop at Mrs. Marshall's—where Lucy's puppy, Venus, was staying till she was old enough to leave her mother next week—and a little love and a cuddle and a pet, Lucy raced home. She changed into some jeans and a T-shirt before she twisted her newly shorter hair into two braids again. It was better to keep it out of her face while she rode. After securing a daisy-tipped holder at the bottom of each one, she was ready when Serena and Mrs. Romero pulled up to get her.

On Lucy's way out the door, Mom handed her an egg salad sandwich to eat in the car.

When Lucy got in, Serena's mom asked, "Would your mom like to come today?"

Lucy smiled. "I'll check!" She ran back inside. "Mom! Serena's mom wants to know if you'll come!"

Lucy saw the struggle on her mom's face. She knew her mom had a deadline this week and was behind. But she also knew her mom was lonely for friends here, too.

"Sunday's a day of rest, right?" Lucy offered hopefully.

Mom smiled. "I'll work double hard tomorrow." She slipped on some tennis shoes, and after telling Dad, they ran to the car holding hands.

Lucy scarfed the sandwich on the way. "I can't wait to tell Carla about the plan."

Serena glowed. "It's such a great ranch, such a great

plan. How can they say no? It'll make a great commercial, and the ranch will be saved. Yahoo!"

Lucy smiled. It was so great to see Serena happy again! Pretty soon they pulled through the open arms of the Double C gate and stopped next to the barn.

When they got out, Brad, the ranch hand, met them. "Carla's gone to town for just a few minutes," he said. "She'll be back, and you can ride if you like."

The moms decided to sit on a wooden bench and chat while the girls rode horses, despite the girls' pleas that they ride, too.

"I'll ride later, I promise," Lucy's mom said.

Has Mom ever ridden a horse? Lucy wondered. She couldn't remember. Her mom was not really the outdoors type.

Brad led them into the barn. Lucy smelled the soft hay, the dry dust, the tang of animal sweat. She walked to the back and peeked out. "What's back here?"

"The stallions," Brad said. "They have their own stalls and paddock to ride in."

Lucy looked up at the two stallions. They were a lot bigger than she thought they'd be, almost like beasts and not animals. One was shiny black and the other rusty with white stars. Handsome. "Are they dangerous?" Lucy asked.

"Well, they're a bit stronger, but Carla has trained them well. As long as you know what you're doing and they're not out with the mares, they're fine."

"Lucy!" Serena called to her. "Do you want Cinnamon or Sugar?"

Lucy walked back to her friend and saw the excitement written on her face. She couldn't break that bubble. Not today.

"Which do you like?" Lucy asked.

"I usually ride Sugar."

"Then I'll take Cinnamon!" Lucy walked up to the horse, being sure not to startle her, making certain that the horse could see her at all times so she wasn't frightened or afraid.

"Funny thing," Brad said as he lifted down the saddles. "Horses are some of the most powerful animals around, and yet they're the biggest scaredy-cats, too." He petted the mares on their flanks. "I don't get out here 'cept on the weekends to help Carla. Wish I saw them more. They're like old friends."

Serena knew how to saddle up her own horse. "One of the first things Carla taught me when I was a little girl."

Lucy did well with just a little help from Brad. She smoothed the buttery leather of the saddle onto Cinnamon; it fit just right.

"No sores for you, girl," she whispered. She talked quietly to the horse. Cinnamon turned her head and nuzzled Lucy, friend to friend.

The girls rode out. As they passed the moms, Serena called, "If Carla comes back, don't tell her our surprise. Let us tell her, okay?"

Mrs. Romero smiled and nodded. Lucy's mom looked a little white. "Are you okay up there?" she asked Lucy.

"I feel right at home," Lucy said. And she meant it. If she had any money, she'd go into business with Carla and be her partner. Maybe when she grew up she could make a ton of money, pay off this ranch for Carla, and buy one of her own. With horses and cows and even—she giggled at the thought—baby pigs. She'd be a rancher! Yeah. Or a vet.

Lucy followed Serena along the fence line. "She paints it in the fall," Serena apologized for Carla, "when the tourists go home and she has more time."

They rode out toward the mountains, tumbleweeds occasionally rolling alongside them like motorcycle sidecars. Cinnamon seemed to sense when Lucy was comfortable enough to go faster and when she leaned back and wanted to slow down. Lucy leaned forward and twirled Cinnamon's mane between her fingers.

Serena pulled her horse to a stop, so Lucy did, too. "I love this place," Serena said, sighing. "It's like a home to me."

We must help Carla, Lucy thought. *For Serena's sake, too.*

"I'll bet Cinnamon would look good with those little foil things on her," Lucy said, trying to make the conversation a bit lighter.

Serena giggled. "Yeah."

After an hour or so, even Lucy's legs were tired. In the far distance they saw some dust kick up. "Carla must be back!" Serena said. "Do you think you can gallop?"

Lucy caught her breath and nodded. "Let's go!" She

kicked Cinnamon's side lightly, and the two of them took off.

They walked into the stables and watered and brushed the horses. Lucy found an apple in a tin bucket hanging on the wall and held it out to Cinnamon. Her leathery lips tickled Lucy's palm as she nibbled it up.

When they were done, Lucy and Serena linked arms and walked into Carla's office. Carla had a pretty jean shirt on today, with double *C*s embroidered on the pocket.

Lucy nudged her friend. "You tell her."

"Are you sure?" Serena whispered. "It was your idea."

"Of course I'm sure," Lucy said. "It was *our* idea."

Serena smiled and cleared her throat. "Carla?" she started. All the women turned to look at Serena. "I've got great news."

Carla smiled at her. "You do? Well, lemme have it."

Serena told her all about their riding at Bixson's ranch the day before and how they had been looking for a movie star autograph when they overheard the Reel Filmworks people talking about ranches and needing a place to film. "So we suggested the Double C— and they'll be here Thursday and Friday to make a final decision! With the money from the rent, you can save the ranch."

Uh-oh. Carla wasn't smiling.

"Isn't that great?" Serena finished.

"Well, no," Carla said.

"No?" Lucy could hardly believe her ears.

"No," Carla answered quietly.

Lucy and Serena looked at each other.

Oh no.

Country Cousin Carla

Sunday afternoon and evening . . .

"Carla, what do you mean?" Serena's mom asked.

"Well, I don't want any city folks coming out here with the ranch kind of—-you know, looking like this."

"But," Serena jumped in, "this is the chance to keep the ranch. For you, for Cal, for the Country Cousins. For, um . . . all of us."

Lucy saw Carla waver. Carla folded her arms. "Bill Bixson's ranch always looks so nice. I wouldn't want Cal to be embarrassed by how the Double C stacks up in a competition for being on TV, that's all."

"Carla, the ranch is fine," Brad spoke up. "The animals are the best taken care of around. The place just needs a little spiffin' up, like all working ranches. A bit of paint, some wood repair where the horses've been snackin' on the fences, the stalls and feedboxes. Normal stuff, that's all."

Carla sighed. "You're right, Brad. But you're only here on the weekends, and I can't pay you enough for all you do as it is. It'd be impossible for me to do all the repairs in three days in addition to taking care of the horses and the business."

Brad shuffled a dirty boot toe on the ground. "I could probably get a few days off from the hotel. They've got other groundskeepers, too. I'll come help with the woodwork. Three good days, I could get it done. For free."

Carla drew a deep breath. "You're a gem, Brad, you are."

"I'm helping Hector this week," Mrs. Romero said, "since his secretary is gone. But if I came one or two days, I could sort through the bills and do the office work."

"I could paint the front sign," Lucy's mom spoke up. "I'm sorry I can't help more than that."

"Serena and I could paint the fence!" Lucy said. "You can take care of the horses, and it will all get done!"

Carla smiled, and when she did, it softened the sun-dried lines chiseled into her lean face. "It's not that easy, girls. Even working long days, it'll take too much time. It takes Brad and me a week in the fall to do the fence alone. You'll have to be runnin'. And even then, I just don't know. It'll take all of three days for Brad to get all the wood fixed. And I just don't feel right asking you all to do this. It's too much."

"It's not too much," Serena said. She looked at Lucy, who nodded.

Carla stood silent. She turned and looked at the Country Cousins' pictures on the wall, then the one next to the wedding picture.

"Who's that one?" Lucy asked softly, pointing to the little gap-toothed girl next to the wedding picture.

"That's me," Carla answered quietly. "I was a city girl who saved up my dollar-a-week allowance so I could ride once a month. That's why I let Country Cousins use my ranch half the weeks of the summer for nothin'." She sighed and then put her arm around Serena. "You want this, too, don't you, honey?"

Serena nodded. "I do, Carla. I really do." Serena pulled out the picture of herself as a little girl, the one she'd forgotten to give to Carla yesterday. "Remember this?"

Carla took the picture from Serena's hand and smiled again, cautiously. "I sure do. Well, I guess I'll take a chance and try it your way. I have nothing to lose and maybe everything to gain." She stuck the picture of Serena up on the board with the Country Cousins' pictures. "Okay if I keep it here?"

Lucy watched as Serena nodded, then grinned with delight. Right then Lucy knew that it would be worth it to give the ranch its best chance, no matter how much work was involved.

"You'd best be getting on, though. I've got some real, live, paying customers coming along in a few minutes, and I'd best get their mounts ready," Carla said. "See you at sunup?"

"Sunup it is," the girls agreed. Before they got into the car, the girls shook hands.

"It's a deal," Lucy said.

☂ ☂ ☂

Later that night, Lucy grabbed the stack of church stuff that her mom had set on the steps and carried it up to her room. She set her Bible next to her bed and opened her notebook. She saw the picture of herself, small next to the horse, and today's verse from church written on it. The humiliation verse! She looked at it and tore it out.

"Lucy?" Dad knocked on her bedroom door.

"Yes?"

"I'm here to help with the violets."

"Oh yeah. Come on in, Dad." Lucy had asked her dad, a plant scientist, to help her revive the wilting plant.

"Do you think it was because I was gone all last week?" She touched the plant. One limp leaf lay on her fingers like a sick child's weak hand.

He looked at the withering plant and shook his head. "Nope. Let's see about moving it to get better light."

Lucy walked it over to her windowsill and put it down. She looked at the paper in her hand. "What do you think about all that humiliation business?" she asked.

Her dad looked puzzled.

"In church. About it being best to be humiliated. I hate being humiliated. I think I had enough humiliation at the ranch yesterday. And I remember when someone spit on this boy in school. Total humiliation."

"Ah." He scratched his beard a bit. "Humility."

"That's what I said!"

"Lucy, humiliation is different from humility."

Lucy held her breath. Was she going to get the short, understandable explanation or the long, drawn-out one full of words she didn't understand? The one that took half an hour and lots of illustrations? You never knew.

"Humiliation is when someone puts you down in a rude way," Dad said. "They're not thinking of anyone except themselves, and they think it's funny to hurt someone. It's the opposite of showing respect. That's not what the Bible is taking about. Humility, on the other hand, is when you gently lower yourself, not putting yourself or your wishes first. It's the opposite of pride, and it's a great way to show respect to others and to God."

Lucy smiled. "I see. Thanks!" At least this explanation was short and sweet. And understandable!

She folded the paper up and stuck it into her jeans pocket. "Thanks, Dad," she said.

He kissed her on the forehead and left the room.

Lucy went back to the window to make sure her

plant was cozy for the night. Across the alley she spotted Serena through her bedroom window. It was so cool having Serena's house kitty-corner from their cottage.

Lucy got on the phone and dialed. "Serena?" she said.

"Yeah, it's me." Serena opened her curtain, and they waved to each other as they chatted.

"I'm going to bed right now so I'll have a lot of energy tomorrow at Carla's."

"Me too," Serena said. "This might be one of the most important things we've done all summer. Besides Venus, of course."

Lucy glanced at the picture of her newborn puppy sitting on her dresser. Venus would come home with her next week! She'd have to stop over again for a play date this week, too.

"I'd better get going. We have to get that ranch in top shape!"

"We will," Lucy agreed.

But as she set the phone back on its cradle, she started to worry. There was a lot of work to be done in three days. Maybe more than they could handle. And a half-fixed, half-painted ranch would look goofy, worse than one that had nothing done at all.

A Tough Choice

Monday . . . D Day minus four

In the cool dusty blue of early morning, Lucy twisted two daisy bands around her braids and whispered, "This one's for you, Little Sal." She slipped the red bandanna Sal had given her around her neck; it rested on her T-shirt like a cowgirl necklace.

Serena and her mom picked Lucy up, the steam from the car's exhaust evaporating into the morning. The girls munched breakfast bars and sipped down pulpy orange juice on the way to the Double C. When they got there, Lucy held her breath. Today was the beginning. Friday was the end. The adventure was in the middle.

"Maa-maa," a little lamb called out to Lucy as she strode into the huge barn.

"I'm not your mama, you silly lamb!" She ruffled the soft wool on its confused head and headed toward

Carla's office with Serena and Mrs. Romero.

Serena's mom set right to work straightening the desk and making piles of bills to file. Carla walked back out into the barn with the girls.

"The horses have eaten, and I think they'll be okay for a little bit, since they'll get some exercise later today. I've let them out into the arena. We need to get the barn tidied up today so Brad can fix the wood in here tomorrow. Also, I'll be having some tourists later today, and I want things to look smart. Serena pretty much knows what to do in here. Start with the saddles, okay?" She looked at Serena, who nodded.

"Just ask me before you do anything different," Carla called over her shoulder as she walked back to the office.

Lucy closed her eyes and sniffed. It smelled like hay and alfalfa, and . . . ugh! What was that?

"That smell," Serena said after looking at Lucy's wrinkled nose, "is what we're scooping up next."

"Gross. Worse than cleaning the bathroom at home." But Lucy grabbed a green plastic shovel, and the two of them mucked out the stalls, tossing the horse manure into a wheelbarrow and then wheeling it over to a stack out of sight at the side of the barn.

Lucy wrinkled her nose. "What happens when this gets too big?"

"Every so often Carla has waste management come and take it all away."

As she wheeled her second load out, Lucy stopped for a minute and stared at the horses. Cinnamon and

Sugar were running around together, and several other mares were standing at the water trough. A baby snuggled between two of them. It must have heard Lucy's wheelbarrow squeak, because it turned and peeked at her through its mother's legs.

So cute! She'd have to ask Carla if the foal could have a treat.

After mucking out the stalls, the girls rubbed the saddles with saddle soap and got them nice and smooth.

"They don't have any shiny buckles on them." Lucy smoothed down Skyrocket's saddle and then turned to Licorice's.

"Right." Serena mopped her head with the small towel she'd brought. Lucy used her bandanna. The thin cracks between the barn boards didn't let in much breeze. "But you notice that the horses don't have any sores on their withers. *These* saddles fit right, and Carla rubs them down regularly. We spent a whole summer once learning how to do that, with the Country Cousins, and how to comb and wash our horses. I think I was eight."

Lucy smiled. "I brought something fun for us to do." She ran to her backpack and brought out strips of tinfoil. "Wouldn't it be cool to put some on Cinnamon and Sugar, just like those pretty ones we rode the other day?"

"Sure," Serena smiled. "Let's finish up here, and then we can bring them a treat and see what happens."

By noon they'd finished a good part of the barn

work, and Serena grabbed the tin pail full of apples. Lucy grabbed the foil.

As they walked across the dusty arena, several horses skittered away, but Cinnamon must have remembered Lucy, because she slowly walked over to her. "Hi, girl," Lucy said softly, being sure to stay where the horse could see her. She drew close and held an apple on her flat palm. Cinnamon nibbled it up, her big, floppy lips tickling Lucy's hand.

Then Cinnamon nickered—a quiet, low, shuddering sound. "That means she likes you," Serena said. "It's horse language for 'You're my friend.' "

Lucy patted the horse. "You're my friend, too." She stepped around and braided Cinnamon's mane, twisting a large piece of foil around each of the ends. The foil caught the sunlight, and spots glinted wherever Cinnamon walked throughout the arena. Lucy handed a few pieces to Serena, who tied them around Sugar's mane.

"Ready for lunch?" Serena asked.

"Yes—but I want to wash my hands first." Mucking stalls was gross! Even though she knew the horses couldn't help it.

The girls ran back to the barn and washed up. Then Serena brought out lunch for both of them— they'd decided that she'd make them a surprise lunch on Monday and Lucy could make one on Tuesday. It would be cool for each of them.

"Let's eat up in the loft," Serena suggested. "It'll be hot, but there are windows we can open."

The girls climbed the shaky ladder to the top, and Lucy brushed straw away from part of the floor for them to sit.

"I've never seen it this empty," Serena said. "Seriously. Carla usually has bales and bales of hay up here, stored for the future."

"Why do you think it's so empty?" Lucy asked.

Serena swallowed. "Money. Maybe she can't afford too much hay right now."

"What will happen to Cinnamon and Sugar if she has to sell the ranch?"

Serena shook her head. "They might get sold. Or if someone buys them with the ranch, they'll keep them. I hope they treat them nicely," she said, her eyes moist.

Lucy sat down next to Serena. "Don't worry. That's not going to happen. We're going to get it all done, and they're going to pay Carla a lot to film the commercials here."

I hope.

Serena opened her backpack and drew out two sandwiches and a bag of chips. Then Serena opened a small bag and brought out a sugar cookie for each of them. "I remembered you like them."

Lucy smiled. "You brought something sugar, and I brought something cinnamon." She opened up her jelly bean case, loaded with Sizzling Cinnamon Jelly Bellies, and passed them to Serena. They both munched.

Lucy already knew what she was planning for

Serena's lunch tomorrow. All of her favorites.

They finished the PB&Js, extra chunky, and then lay back for a short rest. As she did, Lucy bonked her head on something.

She sat up, pulled the straw out of her hair, and reached her hand toward where she had just lay down. "What is this?" Lucy dusted it off and discovered it was a Bible. Inside the cover was written *Cal.*

"Wow! I'll bet Carla doesn't know about this!" Serena said.

Lucy smiled. Carla had been warm toward Serena, of course, and hadn't really been mean to Lucy. But she hadn't been really nice, either. Maybe now that Lucy had found the Bible, Carla would smile at her, too.

They climbed back down the ladder and headed toward the office. They hadn't reached it yet when they heard Carla holler, "What in the good world is flashing out there on my horses?"

Oh no. Lucy watched as Carla ran out and snatched the foil off of Cinnamon and Sugar.

Carla came back into the barn. "What was on those horses?" she asked Serena. She had her back toward Lucy.

"Foil. We saw it the other day at Bill's, and Lucy— I mean, we—thought it would look cute."

Carla turned toward Lucy. "Don't put frilly stuff on my horses." Her voice was as rough as the ranch fences.

"I'm sorry," Lucy said. Carla nodded. Lucy brought out the Bible. "I found this in the loft. While I was eating lunch, I mean; I wasn't being lazy," she said.

She held out the Bible toward Carla, who looked at it and let out a sigh. If Lucy didn't know better, she would have thought that unemotional Carla had a tear in her eye.

But instead of reaching for it, Carla turned. "Just take it back up there." Then she walked away.

The Bible felt heavy in Lucy's hands.

"I'm sorry," Serena said. "I know you didn't mean to do anything wrong with the foil. I didn't think she'd get mad about it."

Non-sobby Lucy held back her own tears. "It's okay," she said. "I'll go put this back in the loft."

Afterward Lucy asked, "Do you want to paint for a little while? It might be a good change of pace."

"Sure," Serena said. "Let's go."

As they walked toward the front gate with two big brushes and a tin of paint, Lucy thought, *It's weird that Carla was so mad at me that she didn't even want Cal's Bible.*

Getting the paint on the fence without dripping all over the place was a lot harder than they had thought. They didn't want the ground to look drippy and sloppy. After a couple of hours, when Carla whistled to them, they had done an amazingly small part of the job.

We're not going to finish in time, Lucy thought. *And a half-painted fence is going to look way worse than an unpainted fence.*

When they got into the office, it sparkled and was extra neat. Mrs. Romero looked tired but happy.

Carla's eyes crinkled around the edges. "You did a good job in the barn today," she said. Lucy knew she was talking to both of them, but she looked at Serena first.

"I don't think we're going to make it in time," Carla continued.

Oh no!

"We could use a little more help."

"Roberto got a job in town," Serena said, referring to her big brother. "So he can't help."

"Actually," Carla said as she mopped her brow, "I was thinking of someone else. You girls will definitely need help painting the fence, and just about anyone could do that. But if we could get someone else who also knew what she was doing with my horses, I could use a little help with them."

"Someone who knows your horses?" Lucy asked.

"Exactly." Carla looked at her and then turned back to Serena. "I was thinking about your friend Julie."

"Julie?" Lucy asked.

"Yes," Carla said. "Is that a problem?"

"Oh," Lucy said. She was careful not to say no, because that would be a lie. But she didn't want to tell Carla yes, because then she'd have to explain. And she knew Julie was at the ranch a lot, and Lucy was new. Julie had made it her business to make Lucy feel as unwelcome as ants at a picnic since Lucy had arrived on the Island. And, she remembered, Julie and Serena had ridden together every summer.

Carla went to answer the phone, and Serena leaned over to say, "I know how Julie has been to you this summer. So you can decide whether to invite her or not. If you don't want to, you and I can maybe get it all done." But she looked doubtful.

Lucy nodded slowly. "We could. Probably."

"Why don't you decide what to do and let me know," Serena said. "We can call her then, if you want to."

Lucy had hoped that this week would be just the two of them, Lucy and Serena, riding together, working together, making things happen for good. If they invited Julie, it would be inviting trouble.

But she could see now that if they didn't ask Julie for help, the work might not get done in time.

A Show or
a No-Show?

Monday evening . . .

Lucy stood over the telephone in her room, hand on the still-hung-up receiver, deciding whether to call. She'd be leaving shortly to go to Power Hour, the youth group at church. They were meeting at the beach tonight for a marshmallow roast and fun time. She'd tried calling Serena to tell her she could invite Julie after all, but Roberto had said Serena was gone and wouldn't be back till it was too late to call.

If Lucy didn't call Julie then and invite her, Julie wouldn't come tomorrow. And there were only a few days left to get it all done.

Lucy picked up the phone, looked at the phone list, and dialed the first two numbers. Then the last numbers. It rang twice before anyone answered.

"Hello?" It was a boy's voice. *Must be Jeffrey, Julie's brother.*

"Hello, may I speak with Julie, please?" *Not that I have any idea what I'm going to say to her.*

"Sorry, she's not here," Jeffrey answered. "She's at the beach. Want me to take a message?"

"No thanks." Lucy breathed a sigh of relief. *I did try, after all.*

She rebraided her hair and put on a fresh pair of jeans. *No sense smelling like a horse tonight,* she thought with a smile.

After packing her Bible and her two-way radio into her beach bag, Lucy slipped on her flower-power sandals, kissed her mom good-bye, and made arrangements for her dad to pick her up at the beach in a couple of hours.

She walked down the street alone. Sometimes Lucy thought it was cool that Serena went to another church and they were still Faithful Friends. Sometimes it felt kind of lonely, though.

Well, you'll have a good time anyway, she told herself.

She got to Crescent Beach, where everyone was supposed to meet. She spotted the leaders over near a picnic table, setting up some drinks. They waved as they saw Lucy approach. She waved back. *Thank goodness they remember who I am after I was gone for camp last week.*

"Can I help?" Lucy asked.

"No thanks! We're just getting the refreshments set

up. We're going to have a sand castle–building contest before roasting marshmallows. You can go find someone to build with if you want."

Hmm. Lucy scanned the beach and saw Erica's flyaway hair in the distance. Erica! She could build with Erica. Lucy ran down the beach, sand flying behind her. As she got closer, she saw Amy next to Erica.

Erica must have invited her. Sometimes it felt weird when you budged in on best friends.

"Hi," Lucy said. She stood close but not too close.

"Hi, I'm glad you're here!" Erica said. Amy smiled, too.

"We're going to build a castle out of sand bowls," Erica said. "A mermaid house—you know, something kind of girly. Amy collected some shells for windows. Those guys are doing something from outer space." She jerked her thumb toward the boys a few feet away.

Jake looked up and saw her. "Hey, Dr Pepper," he called out and waved. Lucy blushed but held her own.

"Hey yourself, Chief," she called back. His dad called him Chief. Jake smiled, and the wrinkles along his tan face made him look older than almost thirteen. Serena had said his birthday was right after school started.

"Do you want to build with us?" Amy asked. Lucy looked at Erica's face to see if it bothered her.

"Are you sure? I mean, I don't want to intrude."

"There's always room for three." Erica scooted over. "Unless you'd rather go over there and build with them." She pointed toward Jake.

"No thanks!" Lucy giggled. "I'm glad you invited me. I haven't built a sand castle in a long time. It's kind of fun." She scooped along with them.

After they had patted the sand into a mermaid house, Lucy walked down to the water's edge. She was looking for something important, something comical to give their house a funny touch.

Jake came down to the water, too. "How are the horses going?"

"Fine," she said. "We're out there painting this week. Getting it all spiffy for Carla."

"She's great," Jake said. He kicked the surf a little. "Her husband was really nice, too. He died from cancer a couple of years ago."

Lucy nodded, remembering his Bible. "Was he a Christian?"

Jake smiled. "Yeah. He went to Serena's church. Played guitar there." Jake played a fake guitar in the air. Lucy shook her head. Boys were diffcrent. Even nice boys.

"I'd better get back to helping with the spaceship. No grain, no gain, you know. Get it—grain of sand?"

Lucy giggled at his painfully bad joke. "Okay," she said. "See you later."

She kicked the surf where Jake had stood, and something brushed against her foot. A whole little crab shell. Dead, of course.

She held it away from her so she didn't have to breathe in the rotten smell and walked back to Amy and Erica. "Here. A doorman for our house."

Erica giggled and posted the crab outside. "Okay, so maybe we'll win after all."

Everyone walked around and looked at one another's castles. Besides Spaceship Catalina and the Middle Island Mermaid, there were also a boat and a kite and a simple sculpture of their little white church.

Even though it was the simplest, the church won almost everyone's vote. Not because it was the fanciest, but because of what it stood for. The ones who had built it looked embarrassed to have won.

Humility, Lucy thought. And indeed, the leaders talked about the very same passage on humility that the pastor had spoken on yesterday.

They all sat around the campfire and prayed and sang. Amy looked like she felt kind of strange. Lucy knew she wasn't a Christian, but Erica kept trying to bring her to church things. *Go, Erica!*

Lucy told them that she was working at Carla's ranch that week with Serena. "There's so much to do."

Hey! I know! I should ask them if they want to come and help. It would be so much fun, Lucy thought.

But . . . Carla hadn't said that she could invite anyone else. Just Julie.

"Sounds fun," Erica said. "We're going to Disneyland tomorrow to have some fun of our own. Amy's mom and dad are taking us for a few days."

"Oh, cool," Lucy said, flexing her pink toes like little crab claws digging into the sand. *So they can't help anyway.*

After they toasted marshmallows Lucy began to

look toward the top of the beach for her dad, who was going to pick her up so she didn't have to walk home alone in the dusk.

Erica and Amy left, and then Jake. Lucy kept scanning. She spotted someone she knew all right, but it wasn't Dad.

It was Julie.

If she walks the other way, I don't have to say anything, Lucy thought. But Julie kept walking closer to her, alone.

Her brother had said she was at the beach. But why did it have to be this beach? There were three beaches in Avalon, after all.

Please, God, let there be some other way to let this happen except to ask Julie.

Nothing came.

Lucy drew a deep breath and walked toward Julie. Julie saw her and stopped. She tossed her long, pretty mane in the wind and looked Lucy over. Whenever Lucy stood next to Julie, she could feel Julie's power.

Lucy walked toward her. "Hi, Julie."

Julie nodded but didn't smile. "Hi."

"I . . . I have a favor to ask you," Lucy began.

Julie raised her eyebrows.

"I don't know if you know, but Carla's ranch is in financial trouble," Lucy began.

"How would *you* know?"

Lucy felt anger burning under her skin. "Because she *told* me." *Cool off,* she told herself. "Anyway, Serena and I are out there cleaning up with her this week, because there's a possibility that a commercial might get to be filmed there, and then there would be some money for Carla."

"So what's the favor?" Julie asked.

"Well, Carla thought you might be willing to come out and help with the work this week. Painting and, um . . . taking care of the horses."

It hurt to get those last words out. If only Lucy were able to be better with the horses. She did love them, after all.

Julie said nothing for a minute. Then, "I don't think I want to come and hang out if you and Serena are being all buddy-buddy."

"You could bring Jenny or something."

"Jenny's not home yet," Julie said.

Why isn't there another way?

"Well," Lucy echoed Erica's words earlier that evening. "There's always room for three."

Julie snorted. "If I *do* come, it will be to help Carla. Not you." She started walking away and then turned around. "I'll think about it."

After she left, Lucy felt as hot and shaken as the hornet's nest Brad had removed from the fence line that morning. On the other hand, she also felt stung.

"It's not like you couldn't help me with this, God," she said under her breath. "I'm doing my best. At least you could have made her be nice to me for once!"

Lucy looked back at the beach and at the little sand church, the only sand sculpture still standing. Then she looked away, as if she didn't want to look at God's face right now or have Him look at hers. Realizing that only made her feel worse.

Just as Lucy's dad pulled up, she saw Julie hop onto a bicycle built for two with her brother.

Will she show up tomorrow or not?

Stranger at the Gate

Tuesday . . . D Day minus three

Lucy rubbed her eyes and blinked over her whole-wheat English muffin with peanut butter. A shower would wake her up. Yeah.

"Remind me to get a job where I can sleep in when I grow up," she muttered as her mom started the coffeepot.

"I guess that means no ranch for you," her mom joked. "Better try plan number two. We'd better get going. This is the only day I can help Carla, and I'd like to get the sign painted. I'll call Mrs. Marshall, and we can stop on the way home and visit Venus if you want."

At that Lucy perked up a little. She slid her plate into the sink just as the telephone rang.

She and her mother looked at each other. It was pretty early to be getting calls. After the second ring Mom answered.

"Hello?" She paused a second before continuing. "Yes. She's right here."

Mom held the phone out to Lucy. Lucy mouthed the words, "Who is it?" and her mom shook her head.

"Hello?" Lucy said.

Someone cleared her throat on the other end. "Lucy, this is Julie."

Lucy woke up totally, fast. "Oh. Hi."

"Hi. Well, I decided I want to help Carla." Lucy could hear someone coughing in the background. It sounded like Julie's mom.

"That's great."

"Yeah, well, my mom, um . . . can't take me. So I was wondering if you could pick me up."

Lucy heard humility in Julie's voice. She'd never heard it before.

"Sure," Lucy said. "We'll be there in about forty-five minutes, okay?" Lucy knew where Julie lived, having visited for one brief minute a few weeks back, after her birthday party.

"Bye." Julie hung up without saying thanks.

Lucy showered and slipped into the jeans that she'd worn last night. The other ones still needed to be washed. After doing her hair, she went down to make the lunches.

First, bologna and mustard sandwiches. Roberto had told Lucy that Serena secretly loved bologna and mustard, so Lucy had bought some yesterday. Lucy didn't really like mustard, but she'd eat it with a smile this once for her friend.

After making and packing two, she thought, *Will Julie remember to make a lunch?*

Lucy slipped two more slices of bread out of the bag and smoothed mustard across one and mayo across the other. She added a couple of slices of bologna, made a quick cut, and wrapped it in waxed paper.

She tossed some carrots into a large bag—*Horse food,* she thought with a giggle—and some chips. For dessert she'd been planning to bring some peanut butter cups, Serena's favorite. But Lucy had only bought two packs yesterday.

She unwrapped each package and slipped out the four candy cups. She left one in the fridge for her dad and put the other three into the cooler. Her mom put her salad and sandwich in the cooler, too, with the water.

Then they were off in the university's Jeep.

They picked up Serena first but not her mom. Today Mrs. Romero had to help her husband, who was working from home, but she waved from the doorway and kissed Serena on both cheeks as she left. The streets were still quiet when they picked up Julie. Julie's house was dark. No one kissed Julie good-bye at the door.

Once they arrived at the ranch, Carla shook hands with Julie. "Why don't you see what's happening with the animals," Carla said to Julie. "Serena and Lucy can finish up in the tack room, making sure the barrels are tidy, the harnesses all where they're supposed to be. They got confused last week with the little ones here. And then you can paint the fence."

Carla finished, "When you're done working, you can ride. If you have any questions about the horses, just ask Julie what she thinks."

Then Carla left.

"Okay, you two into the tack room. I'm going to take care of the animals," Julie ordered. "I'll come and check on your work in a few minutes." Julie walked back to where the stallions were kept.

Mama mia. Of course she'd go toward the stallions first, Lucy thought. *I'm going to ride one of them. Today.*

Serena put her hands on her hips. "Well, it looks like *someone* has her bossy boots on today," she said. The girls headed back to the tack room, where they'd oiled and soaped the saddles the day before.

The floor of the tack room was concrete. On the walls were nailed half-barrels, two high. In the barrels were the harnesses and saddles for the horses, whose names were painted on the outside of the barrels. Kind of.

"Maybe my mom can come in here and paint them, too," Lucy said as she pointed to the barrels. "They look kind of tacky."

Serena giggled. "Tacky? In the tack room? That's a good one."

Lucy giggled, too. They were still together, having a great time, even if Julie was here, too. As they cleaned up, they told as many bad jokes as they could think of, laughing all the while.

"Why did the horse buy a brush?" Serena asked.

"I give up."

"She wanted a ponytail."

"Oh no," Lucy said. "I learned my lesson. No more pretty horses." They laughed again.

After a couple of hours, Lucy went to bring something up to the loft and saw Julie brushing one of the horses—Ned or Red, Lucy couldn't remember which. Julie spoke to it softly. Lucy couldn't decide if she was jealous that Julie got the good job or astonished that Julie was being soft. She'd only seen Julie be soft with her friend Jenny.

"We're going to eat lunch," Lucy said to her. "Do you want to come with us?"

Julie froze. "Um, no thanks."

"I made lunch for you," Lucy said. "I made one for all of us."

"Oh," Julie answered. "Well, okay. Thanks."

The three of them sat in the loft and ate.

"Mustard and bologna!" Serena screamed. "My favorite!" She hugged Lucy, and Lucy and Julie looked at each other over Serena's shoulder. Lucy could tell by Julie's face that she didn't think mustard and bologna were so hot, either. Each of them almost cracked a smile.

After a peanut butter cup each, Lucy hoped the day would go sweeter.

Nope.

Julie finished up her food and started right in again. "You two clean out the feed stall while I bring the horses in." Julie wrapped up her garbage and headed down the ladder.

The girls cleaned up around the feed trough, and Julie rode the horses in. "Tie them up, would you?" she told Serena.

She didn't ask me, Lucy thought. *I could tie them up, I really could.* Should she do it, though? It's not like Carla told them to *obey* Julie, after all.

But she didn't, for now.

"I'm *not* tying Sugar up yet," Serena said, her stubborn chin toward the sky. "Let her walk around and have some freedom."

Lucy wasn't sure, but she didn't say anything.

The other horses were at the feeding trough, and Julie walked another one in. "Better tie them up."

"Hmm." Serena did tie up the new horse, and when she turned, she saw that Sugar was cramming her way in between the two horses feeding.

"Sugar! No!" Serena called. Her loud voice startled the horses and they jerked back, though they were still tied to the feeding trough.

As they pulled back, their reins tugged on the trough. All that massive horsepower! In one giant crash the trough pulled off the wall and spilled feed onto the floor.

"Oh no!" Serena said. Brad came running in.

Serena was near tears.

"I can fix it," Brad said with a sigh. "But it'll pull

me away from the fences for a while."

Julie brought the last horse in, looking really angry. Lucy moved closer to Serena. "It's okay," Lucy said. "We've got to paint the fences now anyway."

Serena nodded. Julie went to tell Carla that the horses were all inside so they could paint that area of fencing without the horses getting wet paint on themselves. Lucy and Serena took the paint cans and brushes outside.

"I guess I should have listened to Julie, Bossy Boots or not," Serena said.

"Yeah," Lucy agreed. "But it'll be okay."

"I just wanted to be with Sugar. And to give her a little freedom. Now Brad has to fix that and we might not get done."

"Let's paint like crazy!" Lucy said. "We'll get done, and then if we can help Brad somehow, we will."

But after Julie came back, she sent Lucy to the far end of the fence to paint by herself while Serena and Julie painted together.

Lucy was going to say something but decided this time she'd let Julie direct. Maybe she knew something Lucy didn't about this. Though Lucy couldn't imagine what it was.

As she looked at the road, she saw a big black truck drive by. Its windows were tinted black, too, so you couldn't see inside. It pulled up in front of the Double C and stopped.

Lucy looked at the gate. She wished her mom were still out there painting the gate, but she wasn't. She'd finished and had gone in to paint the barrels in the tack room.

The truck went up the road, and Lucy breathed easier. She got back to painting.

A few minutes later, though, the truck stopped at the gate again. Lucy looked—Serena and Julie were far away. Laughing together, it looked like.

Lucy's mom was in the tack room, and Carla was in the office. Brad was in the barn.

The black truck didn't move, and suddenly it seemed spooky that she was out there all alone. Finally it slowly drove away.

8

Decisions

After the unsettling time with the mysterious black truck the day before, Lucy didn't feel like spending time alone at the farthest reaches of the ranch.

When they arrived at the ranch the next day, Lucy asked, "Can we all work together today?" It was more fun with others anyway.

"Okay," Serena said. Julie didn't answer.

First they went to the fences. Carla was taking care of the horses herself this morning—she'd finished all of her paper work.

Lucy smiled when she heard that. Brad was finishing up the woodwork today, too. It looked like they just might make it on time.

"The horses could use some exercise," Carla said.

Yes! Today was the day, Lucy thought. With everything going on and Serena so wanting to ride Cinnamon and Sugar, Lucy just hadn't had the heart to bring up her secret wish—to ride the stallions. *After today, though, our Diary Deed will be just like the diary girls.*

As she walked into the barn to get the paint cans, she patted the little lamb on the head and got out of the way while two piglets chased each other. Carla was in the tack room, sweeping out the cobwebs.

Lucy grabbed the paint and walked over to the paddock where Licorice and Skyrocket stayed, separate from the mares. Stallions were okay, she remembered, as long as they were kept away from the mares. Last summer Lucy wasn't ready to ride a stallion. But she was now, especially since she'd been on Cinnamon a few times in the last couple of days.

Skyrocket looked especially exciting. Lucy smiled to herself. *I like a good challenge.*

"He's a beautiful horse, isn't he?" Carla came up behind Lucy.

"Yes," Lucy answered. "He's just like Black Beauty. Only better."

With that, Carla smiled her first warm smile at Lucy. "I see the fence is nearly done. Good job." Carla turned then and went back to check on a horse's shoe.

Totally motivated now, Lucy grabbed her paint and ran to meet Serena and Julie outside. They painted and painted, stopping only to sip water. The grasses around them hummed with a symphony of bugs; a troupe of crickets were startled off stage as the girls moved farther down the fence line.

"Hey!" Lucy remembered. "I have a few more jokes for you." She and her dad had looked them up on the computer last night after she'd told him about her "tacky" joke.

"Okay!" Serena said. "Shoot."

"What disease do horses fear most?" Lucy asked.

Serena shook her head, and Julie kept hers down. It didn't look like she was interested in chatting.

Lucy sighed. It never felt good, even if you knew what kind of person was snubbing you.

"Hay fever!" Lucy finally answered. Serena giggled.

"One more," Serena said.

"Okay." Lucy perked up. "This one is a story: The other day I went horseback riding. Everything was going fine until the horse started bouncing out of control. I tried to hang on, but I was thrown off. Just when things could not *possibly* get worse, my foot got caught in the stirrup. I fell headfirst to the ground. My head continued to bounce harder since the horse didn't stop or even slow down. Just as I was giving up hope, the store manager came and unplugged the horse."

Serena burst out laughing, and Lucy did, too. She stopped, though, when she thought she heard Julie snort.

Maybe she was snorting at the joke. Maybe she didn't mean it to be mean. Lucy didn't feel like any more jokes right then, though.

Finally they finished painting! Lucy looked over the polka dot drips on their shirts and the dusty swipes on their skin. But the fence—it looked fantastic!

They ran in to tell Carla, who gave them a thumbs-up. "We might just get this work done, thanks to you girls," Carla said.

Julie asked Carla if she could eat lunch with her, and Carla said yes.

"Do you feel bad not asking Carla if we should eat with her, too?" Lucy whispered. "Like, leaving Julie all alone?"

Serena shook her head. "No. I think Carla is kind of like an aunt to her or something. Especially since Julie's mom isn't home too much. She works a lot of hours. I think she's glad to have some time with Carla to herself."

"Oh." So maybe that was why Julie was so rude when Lucy knew the ranch was in trouble and Julie didn't.

Anyway, Lucy was glad for the chance to eat lunch just the two of them.

They crawled up into the still, stark loft, bare to the floorboards. There wasn't going to be much hay for the horses. The feed bags looked thin, too.

Serena said, "I used to eat up here a lot during the summers. It was kind of my private spot. But it's much more fun with you."

"Thanks for sharing all your special places here with me," Lucy answered. *I want to keep them for you, too,* Lucy thought. *And the Country Cousins.* After unwrapping the cheese sandwich her mom had made for her, Lucy took a bite. They sat quietly together, resting.

Suddenly she heard something rustle in the far corner of the barn.

Serena must have heard it, too. "Mice?" she asked, a look of disgust on her face.

"I don't know," Lucy said. "I'll look."

Serena looked relieved but moved a bit closer to the ladder.

Lucy tiptoed over to where she'd heard the rustle. The noise stopped. There was more hay way back here. It tickled her nose a little, and she sneezed.

When she did, there was the rustle again, and this time she could see where it was coming from.

She bent over, ready to leap back if the mice scattered, but what she saw wasn't mice at all.

"Ooo," she said. "Serena, come here. It's kitties!"

Serena came over.

First Lucy petted the mother cat, who was wary. She scratched behind her ears. "Don't worry, little mother cat. I may be a city girl, but I love animals," Lucy whispered. After a few minutes the mother cat relaxed, and Lucy reached her hand down and scooped up one of the two kittens.

She handed the first one to Serena. "Thank you," Serena said. She cuddled it close to her face.

Lucy took the other kitten but knelt down beside the mother cat so she could see she wasn't taking the kitten far.

They played with them a few more minutes and then returned to their lunches.

"No wonder we haven't seen any mice," Lucy said.

"Mother cat's been getting them for her babies."

Serena smiled. "You know what it kind of reminds me of? I mean the barn and the animals and babies being born here and all, even if they are animal babies and not human babies."

"What?"

"Jesus was born in a barn, too. What is that word again, that he was born in a low place?"

Lucy finished her sandwich. "Humble. Not a very snazzy place for the Son of God."

"Yes, humble," Serena said quietly. Then, "Let's go and ride."

They tumbled down the ladder, and as they got to the bottom, Lucy could see into the stalls where Licorice and Skyrocket were usually tethered. They weren't there. Instead, she caught a glimpse of Carla and Julie out riding them in the stallion paddock.

Lucy tried to smile. And keep her chin up. But after all, she really had wanted to ride them this afternoon.

"Cinnamon and Sugar?" Serena suggested.

"All right," Lucy said. She tromped over to Cinnamon, but once she got there and Cinnamon rubbed up against her and nickered, Lucy couldn't be disappointed. Cinnamon had called Lucy her friend. And tomorrow—with nothing stopping her—Lucy was going to ride the big, bold Skyrocket.

After riding the horses—and taking care to rub them down afterward—the girls were almost ready to go home.

The fence was painted, the gate was painted, and the tack room was tidy. Even the barrels holding the halters and harnesses were neat. Lucy looked out over the ranch.

Yeah, the barn needed a little more tidying up in the morning, but nothing major. They could definitely get it all done before tomorrow afternoon when the producer and location scout arrived. Nothing could stop them now.

As they stepped into Carla's office to say good-bye, they could immediately tell something was wrong.

Lucy wasn't going to speak up first. No way. Not when Carla had just decided to like her.

Serena's mom did, though. "Carla?" she asked. "We're just about to leave. But is something wrong?"

Carla sighed and sat down. She shoved the phone aside; it had been sitting in front of her. "I just got a call."

Uh-oh. Bad news. Lucy could hear it in Carla's voice.

"It was Bill Bixson. He said that he knows I am going to try for the commercial, too. And he says if I don't back out right now, he's going to stop sending his overflow customers to me." She frowned. "What I can't figure out is how he knew we were competing with him!"

Like a flash, the thought came to Lucy. "Does he drive a black truck?" she asked.

"Yeeesss . . ." Carla began.

"Well, a truck drove by yesterday. He slowed way

down and looked at me while I was painting. And he probably saw the gate my mom had just painted." Since her mom was an artist, the gate probably looked a tad more fancy now.

"He saw the girls talking to the film crew last week," Serena's mother explained.

Carla sat silently before continuing. "If I don't pull out and don't win, he'll take his overflow business away and the ranch will be kaput for sure. But if I do pull out, there goes the chance of keeping the ranch long term."

"Bill Bixson is mean!" Julie said.

Both Lucy and Serena turned to look at her. But it was Carla who answered.

"Sometimes he is. But he had a daddy who told Bill he was worthless, and even though his daddy is dead, Bill is still trying to prove himself. I don't agree with his methods, but I understand his feelings. A lot of what I do for the ranch is for Cal."

"And Bill does send some overflow customers here," Serena's mom pointed out.

"Yes, but I don't know if it's out of the goodness of his heart—which is there sometimes, though not this week. Or if he just wants me to know he has more than I do. He certainly has much more money than the Double C."

Serena spoke up, her voice quivering. "What will you do? The producer and location scout will be here tomorrow afternoon."

Lucy looked at her and saw in her face how much she wanted the ranch to be okay forever and ever.

"I don't know," Carla said. "I'll decide by morning."

9

Skyrocket

Thursday morning . . . D Day minus one

The next morning the three girls stood in Carla's office. The ranch was in tip-top shape. Brad had fixed the wood, and the girls had raced through painting and gotten it all done. The barn was tidy except for the morning mucking out. Everything was in place for the producer and the location scout—if Carla agreed to let them come.

Carla stepped into her office. Her ironed jeans and snapped-up jean shirt said as much as her sparkly eyes. "I've decided to give it a try," she said. "I've got nothing to lose, maybe everything to gain. And I'm proud of my ranch and my horses."

All three girls erupted in cheers. Serena and Julie grabbed hands first for just a minute, and then Serena hugged Lucy with a big squeeze.

"Now all that has to happen is they choose us," she whispered.

Lucy smiled. "I hope they will."

Carla cleared her throat. "I'm going to meet the ferry. I've got a small shipment of hay coming in. Can you girls please tidy up the stalls a little and then make sure I've got quick, easy access to the loft for the hay?"

They all nodded and Julie answered, "Sure."

"I should be back in just a little while," Carla said. "And Brad is here if you need anything." Then she hopped into her red truck and drove through the newly painted gate with the kissing *C*s.

As soon as Carla had gone, Julie dusted off her bossy boots. "Lucy, you take care of the stalls, mucking them out and sweeping. Serena and I are going to the loft." With that, she turned and began climbing the ladder.

Serena looked at Lucy. "Is that okay? I think it's just because it takes two people to lift some of the stuff up in the loft."

Lucy nodded, steamed. As soon as they were gone, she thought, *Well, why couldn't we each muck out a stall and then all go into the loft?* Bossy Boots hadn't seen it that way.

She picked up the green scoop shovel and began to clean out the floors behind and underneath the horses. Cinnamon nuzzled Lucy, and Lucy patted her back.

Then she washed her hands, opened her backpack, and popped a few Sizzling Cinnamon Jelly Bellies into her mouth before taking the wheelbarrow full of manure out to the pile.

As she wheeled it past the stallion paddock, she got a glimpse of Skyrocket.

He sure looks calm today, she thought. *Quiet. Maybe even ridable. Serena has ridden a stallion before, after all. I haven't. Tomorrow is D Day, and who knows what will be going on with the producers doing their official testing and all. I might not get another chance.*

As she wheeled the barrow across some boards to the pile, it hit a bump and a big scoop of manure plopped out onto the ground, barely missing her feet. *It isn't fair! Why can't I be in the warm loft with the little kittens and the soft hay, too? And we could all do* this *together.* Lucy stomped back into the barn and got the plastic shovel. On her way out, she petted Skyrocket, who poked his nose through the bar.

He stood still for her.

Lucy walked back out to the accident, cleaned it up and brought it to the pile, and then wheeled back into the barn.

As soon as she was done, she heard Serena and Julie giggling up in the loft.

I've only got a couple more stalls to do, she thought. *I'm going to ride Skyrocket.*

She walked over to the tack room and got Skyrocket's saddle out of his barrel. Then she slipped into the stallion paddock. Both horses were quiet.

They're sure a lot bigger than Cinnamon, Lucy thought as she stood in Skyrocket's huge shadow. *All of Carla's horses are well trained,* she reassured herself.

I'm doing all the icky work today, and I deserve a

reward. If Julie can ride Skyrocket, so can I. I know I'm just a city girl, but I'm a good rider. I've been practicing on Cinnamon all week. Right? And Carla said to ask Julie about which horses to ride only if we had questions. . . .

Lucy touched Skyrocket softly, talking to him and making sure he could see her as she saddled him up. Then she opened the metal gate between the stallion stall and their separate paddock for riding.

I don't have any questions about riding him. She wavered a little, unsure. *Right?*

Lucy mounted Skyrocket. He stood still but turned his head and rolled an eye at her. He stood there for a minute, not moving. Lucy didn't spur him on, unsure of herself for a minute.

Her heart jump-started, but she shook the reins anyway. As she did, Skyrocket walked forward. Once out in his paddock, he began to go fast. Faster than Cinnamon. Lucy held on with her feet, but the more firmly she put her feet into his side, the faster he went.

Out of the corner of her eye, Lucy spied someone. Two someones, actually, near the stallion fence, with their car parked nearby. Even through the blur she recognized one of them.

The location scout for Reel Filmworks! They aren't supposed to be here till this afternoon!

Lucy tried to slow Skyrocket down, but he didn't slow down enough.

I'll guide him over to the water trough, she thought. She'd seen both stallions slow down when they came to drink water.

Lucy pulled the reins hard left, and Skyrocket obeyed. She got him over to the water trough, and he bent his head down to drink.

Before Lucy had a chance to breathe a sigh of relief, however, Skyrocket turned even more sharply to the right. As he turned, he shrugged his shoulders hard, bent low, and shrugged Lucy right out of her saddle.

She landed with a thud—narrowly missing landing in the water trough. When she looked up, the location scout and the other man—he must be the producer!—looked at her, then looked at each other. The scout raised his note pad in front of his mouth, saying something to the producer without Lucy being able to see.

Lucy looked up at Skyrocket, who rolled his big eye at her again. Her blood shot heat through her veins. "Okay, you made your point," she said to Skyrocket in a tense voice. "You're the boss." She rubbed her hip a little and stood up, shaky. As she brushed the dust from her jeans, she saw that the Reel Filmworks people were still looking at her, though they weren't saying anything now. Neither of them smiled.

Lucy grabbed Skyrocket's reins and waited. When he was done drinking, he followed her back to the barn. He didn't need to do anything else. He had taught her what he thought she needed to know.

As Lucy led him back to his stall, she glanced over at the producer and the location scout. They had turned their backs to her.

Sick with sorrow and her head airy with embarrassment, Lucy spoke out to God.

"Couldn't you have helped me with this one little thing?" she whispered. "I mean, I've been doing everything for everyone else. All I wanted was to ride the stallion one time this week. Now they are going to think that the horse is mean and bad and too dangerous for their actors."

Lucy led the quiet Skyrocket into the stall and rubbed him down. She kept talking in a low voice, but to herself this time. "They're not going to bring the commercial here now, are they? They're going to think this is a funny ranch and the people who work here aren't skilled. Like me. I'm the first one who talked with them and the first person to blow it."

Skyrocket nibbled the apple she held out to him. It wasn't his fault, after all. Lucy's insides felt like the cake her mom had tried to make for company once. She'd taken it out of the oven too soon; at first it looked all right, and then, slowly, it sank down in the middle and never recovered.

Lucy sat down outside of the stall.

"It's my fault," Lucy spoke softly to herself. "I rode a horse I wasn't sure I could ride, and I was too proud to ask Julie—afraid to look silly and afraid she'd say no. I should have asked. And now, what if I've blown it for everyone? Those producers will probably think the horses are too temperamental to film here."

As she sat there, Lucy heard a noise from outside the barn. It sounded like a vehicle coming up the driveway. It sounded like Carla's truck.

What Tomorrow Means

Thursday afternoon . . .

Lucy stood up and walked quickly over to the loft ladder, hoping the other girls were still there. One by one, she climbed the rungs.

When she got to the top, Serena and Julie weren't up there anymore. She looked out the open loft window and spied them tidying up the horse arena. Carla's truck was there, with hay in the back. Lucy decided she might as well wait in the loft and help shove the hay where it belonged. Besides, she wasn't ready to face them quite yet.

Cal's Bible. I'd better move it, she thought, *so it doesn't get buried under hay.*

She found it and set it next to her. As she reached into her jeans pocket for a Jelly Belly, her hand touched the piece of purple paper from church last Sunday, with the doodle of the large horse and small girl. And the Bible verse.

Opening the paper brought tears to her eyes. Now she really felt like that small girl, in a very unhappy way.

She read the words she'd scribbled down just a few days earlier. *"Pride ends in humiliation, while humility brings honor." Proverbs 29:23.*

Now that her dad had explained humility to her, Lucy realized she hadn't lowered herself at all, not really. Oh yeah, when it was easy or fun, like painting or stuff for Serena, her best friend. But not when it was hard. She hadn't wanted to ask Julie for anything—not to help with the ranch, not to help her with Skyrocket. She definitely hadn't wanted to humble herself in front of Julie.

Lucy opened Cal's Bible and read over the verse in Proverbs again. Somehow it seemed even stronger read right out of the Bible. She heard Carla and the others walking toward the barn. Lucy shut the Bible and closed her eyes.

"Jesus, I'm sorry I blamed you. I blamed you when Julie wasn't nice to me and when Skyrocket dumped me. I'm sorry. Please forgive me—help me not to mess up anymore, and please let me know how to be and how to act. I'll take a chance and do it your way. Like Carla said, I have nothing to lose and maybe everything to gain. Amen."

Lucy opened her eyes and whispered, "Please let

me know how to do it your way, God."

She stepped down the ladder and stood at the bottom, surveying the barn. It was tidy and clean for the most part. She was glad she'd gotten almost everything done. Lucy had a couple of stalls left to muck out, but they were in the back. She'd get right to it, no matter how low and stinky the job, even if Serena and Julie got the cool jobs. This was Lucy's job, and she was going to do it!

As she walked toward the back stalls, she saw a huge new cobweb up in the corner. Just then, the baby pig bumped her leg and then ran beneath the web.

Lucy giggled. Just like *Charlotte's Web*. She looked at the spider web—it was thin, and she didn't want to knock it down just in case Charlotte was up there spinning! She'd always loved that book.

Hmm. What was that word Charlotte had spun into her web?

Lucy had an uneasy feeling it was important for her to remember. And it was. The answer, like the one spun in *Charlotte's Web*, was simple. When the answer came to her heart and mind, Lucy knew it—*humble*.

The power of God speaking to Lucy, right to her, in a creative way that she knew was only for her, brought tears to her eyes again. Happy tears. This was a double answer. Not only to her question right now, but also to her whispered question in the loft—*"Please let me know what to do."*

Lucy wiped away her tears as Carla, Serena, and Julie came into the barn.

Serena ran up to Lucy. "The scout and producer are here early!"

Lucy nodded. "You guys go help Carla with the hay. As soon as I'm done with the stalls, I'll come up and help."

Serena headed toward the loft. Brad was hoisting hay bales up to the loft, and Julie rushed to stack them neatly.

Lucy tidied up the stalls as best she could, sweeping them down, making sure the troughs were neat. Then she blew a kiss to Skyrocket to show she wasn't mad at him. He swished his tail.

As soon as she finished, Lucy ran up the ladder to help with the hay. Serena gave her a big hug. "Thanks for doing the stalls. We got everything ready up here, and now the horses have more hay. Maybe a *lot* of hay if things go right."

Lucy sighed. *If* things went right.

Carla called Serena down to help with Cinnamon and Sugar. Lucy didn't even feel bad that she didn't get to help with Cinnamon.

I'm helping where I can do the best, she thought, balancing some hay bales. All of a sudden she remembered the kittens.

"Julie!" she shouted.

Julie looked up but didn't answer.

"I've got something to show you, but we have to be careful."

Julie looked wary but came anyway. Lucy led her to the back corner where the kitten family lived. The mother was still there, tucked into the corner with her kittens, looking a bit afraid because of all the commotion in the loft.

"Oooh." Julie's voice was as soft as the kitten fur.

A thought crossed Lucy's mind. *Maybe Julie and I have more in common than I thought.*

Lucy wiped her forehead with Sal's red bandanna. "I just want to make sure we don't crush their little area," she said.

Julie nodded, and for once Lucy felt like the two of them were working as a team.

They got the bale as Brad brought it up to the loft, and while he went down for another, the girls worked together to push this one into a corner. Julie decided where the bales should go and told Lucy what to do without asking her opinion on anything.

Lucy swallowed her pride and did what Julie said.

It took about half an hour, but finally the bales were stacked neatly. And while Julie hadn't put them where Lucy would have, she *was* careful to protect the kittens. That was enough for Lucy.

A car honked outside. Lucy looked at her watch. Her mom wasn't due for another hour!

She peeked out of the barn window. It was one of the ferry vans.

Julie peeked out, too. "My mom!" she shouted.

Julie's mom must work for the shuttle company. And judging by the way Julie flew down the ladder, Lucy knew her mom's showing up was a surprise.

Julie ran out to the van. Her mom got out, lighting

up a cigarette as soon as she stepped out of the van. Her skin had the same deep wrinkles that Carla's did but no tan. She had dark circles under her eyes, but she tossed a quick smile at Serena and Lucy.

"I had a break and thought I'd come and take you home for once," she said. "Would your friends like a ride, too?"

Serena looked at Lucy. "Thank you," Lucy said politely, "But my mom is coming in an hour."

Julie's mom nodded. She rubbed her cigarette into the ground. "Let's go, then."

Julie waved good-bye; she even seemed to be looking at Lucy this time. Then the van drove off.

Lucy and Serena walked back to the barn. "Her mom looks tired," Lucy said.

"She's had a hard life."

Lucy looked at the van pulling out onto the main road back to Avalon. "I'm going to pray for them." And she really meant it.

Serena asked, "What should we do now?"

Lucy knew what Serena would choose. "Let's ride Cinnamon and Sugar for a few minutes."

They went into the barn. Carla was there, and they told her their plans.

"It'll give them a little exercise. I'll ride the others this afternoon. Good to get them warmed up before tomorrow, when they'll be looking everything over for good. More film people will be here. And at Bill Bixson's, of course." Carla frowned, and Lucy remembered Bill's threat to cut off the extra business.

I hope I didn't blow it for her—and for Serena. The ranch means so much to them both. Lucy glanced over at Skyrocket. As she got onto Cinnamon, her conscience troubled her. *I should tell Carla what happened with Skyrocket.*

Well, she would. Right after riding.

"Let's try holding hands while we ride—like team riding," Serena said. Lucy giggled and slowed Cinnamon down. She reached out and grabbed Serena's hand.

They paraded through the arena, Cinnamon and Sugar matching perfectly through their moves.

"Let's race!" Lucy said, sticking her heels into Cinnamon's side. "But *not* holding hands!" Serena won, of course, but Lucy burst out laughing. "That was so great."

After a few more spins around the arena, the girls took the horses back, toweled them off, and brushed them down. Lucy found the carrots she'd brought from home and fed them to Cinnamon, then passed the bag to share with Serena and Sugar, too.

"Thanks!" Serena said. "You're so thoughtful of others."

Serena really was her best friend. Lucy decided to tell her about Skyrocket.

"Serena, I have to tell you something kind of—well, bad. Not thoughtful of others."

Serena set her curry brush down, patted Sugar, and came close. "Go ahead."

This is so hard. "Well, I felt mad that I was doing

the dirty work today, and also I really wanted to ride a stallion, just like the diary girls. And because they're big and strong, and you know, I like a challenge."

Serena nodded.

"So I got on Skyrocket this morning. And out by the trough, he dumped me," she finished.

"Are you okay?" Serena asked.

"Yes. But the producer and location scout saw."

"Oh no."

Lucy looked glum. "Oh yes." She looked up at the spider web. "Remember in *Charlotte's Web*, about humble? I'm learning it's harder than I thought." Lucy sighed. "Now I need to tell Carla."

Serena looked beyond her. "Hey! Your mom just drove up."

Carla met Mrs. Larson at the driveway, and the producer and location scout walked over, too. They all strode into the barn, Lucy's mother heading toward the girls.

"Thanks for the great work," Carla called to the girls. "I'll see you in the morning."

With that, she disappeared into her office with the scout and producer and shut the door behind her.

Serena and Lucy looked at each other. Not only didn't Lucy get a chance to tell Carla—yet—they both knew what tomorrow would mean.

In Carla's Office

Friday . . . D Day!

Serena's mom brought them to the ranch the next morning, picking up Julie on the way. Before leaving the house, Lucy had tucked both the old and the new diaries into her backpack.

What will we have to write? she wondered as she zipped them inside. On their way out of town, Serena's mom drove by Bixson's ranch. The Reel Filmworks van was already parked there; they were going to Bixson's first.

After they arrived at the Double C, Serena jumped out and ran into the barn. Lucy put her hand on Julie's arm.

"Wait a second."

Julie turned to look at her. "What?"

Lucy took a deep breath. It would have been easier to do if Julie had been acting kindly.

"I brought something for you. I mean, Serena and I are wearing them every day. I thought you might like some, too." Lucy held two daisy braid holders in her outstretched hand.

Julie looked at them for a long time. Then she took them from Lucy and tucked them roughly into her jeans pocket. "I don't wear braids," she said.

"Okay," Lucy said. She shrugged off the hurt that had settled around her shoulders. At least she'd tried. Lucy didn't like to wear haircombs, after all. Maybe that's all it was.

They walked into the barn and greeted the animals. Lucy could tell that Carla had been up early, feeding all the horses and doing the mucking out herself. The barn looked perfect.

"It looks just right to win this commercial. Or if not, then it looks good enough to sell," Carla said. Lucy desperately hoped it was the commercial. Today would tell.

Lucy walked over to Cinnamon and let her nibble some carrots out of her hand. Then she petted her some.

"You're a good old girl," she told her. Cinnamon nickered.

The little pig was with its mother and several other little pigs, rolling around on a straw bed in a stall of their own for once.

"Maa-maa," came the call from another stall. The little lamb wasn't used to being in a stall during the day, either. Lucy patted its confused head and that of its real mama, too. In return she got a lick on the hand.

Carla came back into the barn. "The producer and his crew are here! I'm going to saddle up a couple of horses for them, and we'll ride the fence line all the way down. After that, we'll show them what a couple of the other horses can do—maybe the stallions, since they look like 'movie' horses." She grinned.

Lucy moved back, feeling uncomfortable.

The girls stood together in the barn, making sure things stayed in place. Lucy still hadn't had Carla to herself. When would she tell her about Skyrocket? It was important to be honest. But Carla was so busy with the adults right now. Part of Lucy was relieved to put it off. Part of her just wanted to get it over with.

Serena's mom stayed in the office, answering the phone. Even Brad was there, in freshly ironed blue jeans of all things, and his boots brushed—but not new. After Carla and the producer's crew left, he walked around the barn shaking things a little, making sure his wood repairs were good and tight.

The girls brushed the horses. Finally Carla came back in. Lucy looked her over carefully, trying to read her expression. She just couldn't tell.

But Carla walked up to her. "I'm going to have some of the horses ride out in the arena," she said. "I'm going to start with the stallions. You and Serena can ride them out, since it was your idea to invite the crew in the first place."

Lucy swallowed back tears. It was a real honor that Carla was offering her now. But she couldn't risk messing things up now. And besides, it just wasn't right. Lucy looked at her and just barely shook her head no.

Carla looked concerned. "I know you were eager to ride them. I saw the way you've looked at them this week. You'll be safe, Lucy. They're well trained, and they do well—especially if they are together."

Julie and Serena had gathered nearby now. Lucy looked up at the nearly invisible spider web where she'd imagined Charlotte had spelled out *humble*.

She took a deep breath. "Julie is a better rider than I am. She and Serena can ride the stallions out. I'll wait here, and I can ride Cinnamon when it's time to show the mares."

"Suit yourself," Carla said. Then she helped Julie and Serena get the stallions saddled up.

Lucy blinked a few tears from her eyes as she saw them race to the stall. *If I had waited, I could've done it with Serena.*

When the girls rode out into the arena, though, Lucy smiled through her tears. Julie had ponytailed her hair. At the top were the two daisy holders.

Lucy watched from the barn as the girls rode the horses through the arena, weaving in and around cones to show how well they behaved. Skyrocket didn't dump Julie. He obeyed her. And he looked to Licorice for direction.

Afterward they brought the stallions in. "I'll rub them down," Julie said. "You can ride Cinnamon and Sugar together."

She didn't stick around for thanks. She just took off to the stallions' stall.

Lucy saddled up Cinnamon and Serena saddled up Sugar, and they rode out into the arena. Lucy held her breath and prayed. And then she touched her red bandanna. *This is for you, too, Sal, and all the city girls like you and me who love animals and need this ranch to stay open for Country Cousins.*

Cinnamon obeyed Lucy's every command. Lucy leaned toward Serena. "I think these horses sense something important is happening," she whispered.

Serena nodded. "Yes. They're very smart."

The crew seemed to be having a good time, smiling with one another. Carla was with them, and she seemed relaxed, too.

Lucy and Serena finished with the horses and then rode them back into the barn. Lucy dried Cinnamon off. "I'll do Sugar, too, so you can make sure the back barn area is clean before the crew comes."

A few minutes later the crew and Carla arrived in the barn. Lucy smiled at them and got back to work— but not before she noticed that Carla hadn't looked her way.

The producer headed toward Carla's office, and Carla headed toward Lucy. Julie and Serena weren't there. Now was Lucy's chance. She didn't want to do it, but she must. Carla stood there for a minute. Now or never.

"Carla?" Lucy began. Her throat was dry.

"Yes?" Carla put her hand on her hip and stood there, looking impatient.

"I need to tell you something. I know you told us we could ride whenever our work was done. But I tried to ride Skyrocket yesterday, without talking with Julie about it first, because I thought I could handle it."

Carla just stood there.

"I got him out to the water trough, and he dumped me. It didn't hurt me, and it didn't hurt him," Lucy continued. "But the producer and location scout saw me. I'm really sorry."

Carla nodded quietly. "I know they saw you. They've just told me all about it. Now, come on. We need to go to my office. The producer, Mr. James, is waiting for us—you and me."

The Decision

Friday morning . . .

Lucy's heart skipped. *Trouble.*

She trailed after Carla, following in silence to the office. They passed Serena, standing next to Sugar's stall.

When Serena mouthed the words, "What's going on?" Lucy shrugged her shoulders.

Once in Carla's small office, Lucy kept standing. There were only two chairs in there, and Carla sat at the one behind her desk. The producer, Mr. James, sat down in the other chair. The other Reel Filmworks crew members must have been outside or loading their gear back into their van. Was that good or bad?

The producer held his hand out, and Lucy shook it. "Nice to meet you," Lucy said, hoping it wasn't a case of the fly shaking hands with the spider. But the producer smiled, so she relaxed a little.

Lucy used Sal's bandanna to wipe a drop of sweat off her forehead. She glanced at the picture on the still-neat bulletin board of Carla as a little girl.

Mr. James cleared his throat. "Yes. I've just told Carla that we'll be coming back to the Double C to shoot the commercial. We're hammering out the final date now."

It took a minute to sink in. Then Lucy shouted, "Hooray! That's great news." She looked around the office, the door closed. "But . . . why am I in here? I thought I was in trouble."

Mr. James leaned forward. "I told Carla that a number of things helped us make our decision. The ranch is neat and tidy, for sure, but it's also authentic. It doesn't pretend to be anything that it's not. It looks like a real ranch."

A humble ranch, Lucy thought. *Not frilly.*

"That's important to us for this commercial. And," he continued, "there may be quite a few commercials if this works out okay."

Carla smiled, and Lucy did, too.

"Another thing that was important to us was that the animals be well trained," Mr. James continued. "We aren't able to bring animals over; we need to be able to count on the ones right here. Today all of the animals looked terrific. But yesterday my scout and I saw you riding that stallion."

Lucy's heart plunked. "Skyrocket," she said.

"Skyrocket," Carla echoed.

"Yes. Well, I'm sure it didn't feel good—inside or

out—when you were dumped." Mr. James seemed to be holding back a smile. "But the fact that the horse let you off softly and didn't run away and then allowed you to lead him back to the paddock . . . well, that showed me something." He smiled in full now. "I'm a horseman myself."

Lucy was confused. "What did it show you?"

"That was a well-trained horse, gentle but smart. He had spirit—and showed you who was boss—but didn't hurt anyone in the process. And he obeyed afterward. Today, with a stronger rider and his partner horse beside him, he obeyed just fine."

Lucy nodded.

"And," Mr. James continued, "I also liked how *you* handled that. You didn't run off or hit the horse or holler or yell or tug on him. You handled him just right. You've got the makings of a good horsewoman."

Lucy felt a huge smile bursting out. For the first time Carla smiled right at Lucy, too.

"Tell Lucy your idea," Carla urged Mr. James.

Idea?

"Carla told me that you were the one who had originally approached my location scout about the Double C. When I saw how you handled Skyrocket yesterday, I had an idea. We'll be back to film in a week or so. Would you like to audition to be an extra in the commercial? That's why I wanted you in here this morning."

Me? In a commercial? The blood ran to Lucy's face. "I'd love it!" she said. Instantly Serena came to mind.

"But my friend also had the idea. Could she audition, too?"

"Yes," Mr. James said. "The script is being finalized right now, so I'm not certain how many parts there will be. But you can invite her to try out, too."

Lucy said thank-you and ran out to the barn to tell Serena. Carla was going to be paid for the film crew to use the ranch! The Country Cousins could come back! Everything was going to be just fine—*and* Lucy and Serena might get to be in a commercial.

When she ran into the barn, she heard the bleating of the lambs and saw one pig escape its pen, but no Serena.

Julie, however, was just walking out to the van her mom had arrived in.

"Carla gets to keep the ranch!" Lucy shouted. She didn't want Julie to go home without knowing the good news. A broad smile spread across Julie's face. For the first time Lucy noticed that Julie looked as tired as the rest of them. She'd worked really hard these last few days, too.

Lucy stopped in her tracks. It wouldn't really be fair if Julie didn't get to try out, too. But Mr. James hadn't said anything about three girls, and Lucy had felt like she was pushing even asking for Serena.

Lucy closed her eyes. "What should I do, God?"

When she opened them and saw the little pig race by her, she knew. *Be humble and ask for help.*

"Don't leave for just a minute," she said to Julie. If Mr. James said only two of them could try out, Lucy would make sure it was Serena and Julie. But she had to try.

She raced back to the office and knocked softly on the door. Carla opened it.

"Mr. James? There were actually three girls here working this week. I don't know if it would be a problem, but could we all try out for parts?"

Mr. James smiled. "That's fine. I'll see the three of you in a little over a week. Carla can fill you in later."

"Thanks!" Lucy ran out to Julie, who was standing at the van looking impatient. But the daisy holders were still in her hair.

"The producer said the three of us could try out for a part in the commercial if we want," Lucy said. "I think it would be fun—if you want to."

Julie's eyes sparkled, and she gave Lucy a real smile. "Thanks."

Julie's mom kept looking at her watch.

"Carla will fill us in later," Lucy said. Julie slipped into the empty van.

As it drove off, Lucy went to find Serena and to tell her the good news.

But Serena was nowhere to be found.

Finally Lucy decided to climb the loft ladder to see if Serena was there. "Serena?" she called over the hay bales.

"Over here," came the muffled reply. "With the kittens."

Lucy smiled. "Carla got the contract!"

Serena whooped. She set the kitten down, and the

two of them danced around, tossing hay like confetti into the air.

Serena pulled Lucy over to the corner. "Tell me all about it."

"Let me write it in our diary," Lucy said, sitting down, "and you can read it and be surprised." She couldn't wait till Serena read the words about trying out for the commercial.

They dug their best friends' diary and the 1932 diary out of the backpack. Each girl sat down with a kitten in her lap, with the mother cat contentedly purring right beside them. As they opened their diary and began to read, they heard the ladder squeak.

Someone was coming up.

Carla!

"Thanks to the two of you—and Julie and Brad and your moms—things are looking okay around here. Cal would be proud. His clean, nice, non-frilly ranch." She cleared her throat. "I'm wondering if Cal's Bible is still here. I . . . I think I'm ready to look at it again now," she said softly.

Lucy took it from the safe place she had set it yesterday when they were unloading the hay. She brushed it off and held it out to Carla. This time Carla took it from her.

"Thank you," Carla said, her face softening.

"You're welcome," Lucy said. "And thank you for keeping a ranch like this for kids who love animals, kids like the Country Cousins. Kids like me."

"And kids like me," Carla said, smiling at Lucy.

"When you're done with whatever you girls are doing, come on down and I'll help the two of you ride the stallions."

"Together?" Lucy asked.

"Together," Carla promised.

Yes!

"What about Mr. Bixson?" Serena asked. "Will he be mad at you?"

Carla chuckled. "Yes—for a while. Then he'll want me to come and help him do something at his ranch. He'll call me up and we'll be friends again. I need to remember that Bill's bark is always worse than his bite."

Serena smiled, and Carla stepped down to the barn. Lucy opened their new diary. Serena scribbled in how thankful she was about the ranch being saved and how fun it was to keep working on good things together, all the time, as Faithful Friends.

Then it was Lucy's turn.

Dear Diary, she began, with Serena looking over her shoulder. *We're going to be famous! Well, maybe. We get to try out for the commercial—all three of us. Not next week, but the week after. Can you imagine if one or more of us gets a part?*

Serena grabbed the book. "*What* did you write?"

Lucy giggled. "You read it right! Isn't that totally cool?"

"Totally," Serena agreed. "That is *so* cool."

Lucy took the diary back and wrote about how God took something bad and made something good from it. And then Lucy sketched a cobweb into the diary, like Serena had shown her how to doodle. She wrote the word *humble* in the web.

She looked up at Serena. "It'll take me a few minutes, but I really want to write this in."

Serena nodded.

God's been teaching me, Lucy wrote, *about lowering myself just a little to serve others and waiting for Him to lift me up, at just the right time, in just the right way. Carla took a chance on our plan, and it worked out just fine. I took a chance and did it God's way after messing up. It worked out just fine. In fact, it feels great. Thank you, Jesus.*

Serena opened up the old diary, and Lucy leaned over her shoulder as Serena began to read.

"Well, we did ride those stallions, Diary. Mary got us on them—as she said she would. We had a wrangler come out and hold the reins for us, but—oh my! It was a tall horse and strong. I'm not sure I'd like to do that again. I'd better stick with bicycles."

Serena handed the diary over to Lucy, who read Mary's section.

"It was great fun, Diary, and we laughed in spite of ourselves. I do like a dare, you know. But since she's done this with me, I'll put up with her plans for next week, Diary. Wait till you see what she's got cooked up for us—for our

whole families, actually. Till then, ta-ta.
Love,
Mary and Serena,
faithful friends."

Lucy closed the old diary. Their best friends' diary was still open. "Okay," she said. "I drew the doodle in the diary this time—not that it's as good as any of yours, you artist. But now *you* have to figure out what to put inside."

"Oh, you're much better at ideas," Serena said. "Let's work together." She pulled a piece of hay from her jeans. "How about something out of hay?"

Lucy closed her eyes for a minute, then snapped her fingers. "How about this?" She took the piece of hay from Serena and pulled one off of her own pants and made them into a cross. Then she took a third one from near the mother cat and twisted it around the middle of the cross, binding it together.

"A humble cross," Lucy said.

"Perfect!" Serena said, closing it into their diary.

As they went down the ladder toward the stallion stall, Lucy asked, "Why was the foal coughing?"

"Why?" Serena asked, puzzled.

"Because he was a little hoarse," Lucy laughed. "The last bad horse joke, I promise!"

And the two of them raced, giggling, toward Sky-rocket and Licorice, where Carla waited to take them for their long-anticipated ride.

For the proud will be humbled,
but the humble will be honored.

LUKE 14:11

The last horse SANDRA BYRD rode was a lovely old chestnut named Ranger—who was gentle and patient and wasn't by any means a stallion!

Sandra lives near beautiful Seattle, between snow-capped Mount Rainier and the Space Needle, with her husband and two children (and let's not forget her new puppy, Duchess). When she's not writing, she's usually reading, but she also likes to scrapbook, listen to music, and spend time with friends. Besides writing THE HIDDEN DIARY books, she's also the author of the bestselling series SECRET SISTERS.

For more information on THE HIDDEN DIARY series, visit Sandra's Web site: *www.sandrabyrd.com*. Or you can write to Sandra at

Sandra Byrd
P.O. Box 1207
Maple Valley, WA 98038

**Don't miss book eight
of The Hidden Diary,
One Plus One!**

For a preview of Lucy and Serena's next diary
adventure, just hold up this page in front of a mirror.

More than ever, only-child Lucy wants a
brother or sister. Serena has her brother, Roberto, and even Claudette has a new little sister
from China. To make matters worse, Catalina's annual brother/sister tandem bike event
is approaching. But Lucy has no sibling to
participate with her. Will she have to sit this
one out?